Weekly Reader Children's Book Club presents

Hotel for Dogs

Hotel for Dogs

LOIS DUNCAN

Illustrated by Leonard Shortall

1971
HOUGHTON MIFFLIN COMPANY BOSTON

For my Arquette nieces and nephews
Debra, Sheri and Rick
Kim, Kris and Kevin
Jim and John
Kelly and Kirk

Hotel for Dogs

Chapter One

THE HOUSE WAS white and square and too small and too perfect.

Bruce studied it from the car window. "Do you suppose there's really room for all of us?" he asked skeptically.

"It looks smug," Liz said. "It has a stuck-up look, as though it thinks it's too good for ordinary people. Even the grass looks fake. I bet it's made of plastic and comes in rolls at the dime store."

"Liz, that is *enough!*" Mr. Walker turned the car into the driveway and came to a stop, but he did not turn off the motor. "You have been acting this way for four days, ever since we left New Mexico. We're here now, and in another minute you are going to meet Aunt Alice. I don't want one more unpleasant remark — not *one.*"

"Just remember how lucky we are, dear," Mrs. Walker added. "Nobody wants to rent a house to a family who may only be living in a town for a short time. If Dad's aunt didn't live here and hadn't been nice enough to invite us to stay with her, we might have had to stay behind. You wouldn't have wanted that, would you?"

"Yes," Liz muttered, but she said it under her breath. She did not want to push her luck too far. Besides, she knew she was being unfair and was a little ashamed of herself. The two-story white house in front of them was a perfectly nice place. Actually, some people might have preferred it to the sprawling old adobe they had left behind them.

The truth of it was, it was not the house itself that she resented. It was the fact that Bebe would not be allowed to live in it with them.

Until she had discovered that, she had been almost as excited about the idea of moving as Bruce. Their father's assignment to a new branch of his company meant a big promotion, and they were proud of him and pleased that he was going to Elmwood for a training program. New people, new experiences, a car trip all the way across the country to the east coast — how could they *not* have been delighted about those things!

And then their mother had broken the news. She had done it in what Liz thought was a very sneaky way, remarking casually in the middle of packing, "I talked to the Cairds about keeping Bebe while we're in Elmwood. They say they would be glad to have her."

"Keeping Bebe!" Liz had repeated the words in bewilderment. "What do you mean?"

"We won't be able to take her east with us, I'm afraid," Mrs. Walker had said. "Your father's Aunt Alice is terribly allergic to dogs."

"We can't take Bebe!" Liz had stared at her mother incredulously. Surely, she must be joking! Still, this was hardly the sort of thing you joked about. "But Bebe's part of the family!"

"She's only a dachshund," Bruce remarked. He was bent over his suitcase, trying to arrange his camera equipment so that nothing could get broken. "That's hardly even a dog. It's more like a noodle."

"It's dog enough for people who are allergic to animals," Mrs. Walker said. "I'm sorry, Liz. I know how you feel, but there's just nothing we can do. Bebe will have a good time at the Cairds'. Kim and Katie will take good care of her."

"She can't stay here! I won't go without her!" Liz had run to Bebe, who was watching all the excitement with interest, and snatched her up in her arms. "If Bebe stays, I will too!"

"Now, dear, don't be ridiculous," her mother had said firmly. "As soon as Dad is through his training and we know where he will be working, we'll find a place of our own and send for Bebe. I'm sure I will be just as glad to see that day come as you will." And she gave a little sigh.

"I won't go without you, Bebe darling!" Liz had

cried miserably, but, of course, when the time came, she had. When you are ten years old you go where your parents go, and that is all there is to it.

Now Mr. Walker turned off the engine and opened the car door.

"Out you hop," he said, "and no more sulking. Put on a pleasant face to meet Aunt Alice."

It was at that moment that the door of the house flew open and Aunt Alice herself came rushing out to greet them. Bruce was the first one out of the car, and so he was the one Aunt Alice grabbed first.

"So this is my darling little great-nephew!" she cried, hugging him to her. "I haven't seen you since you were a baby, and here you are, almost grown up!"

Bruce, who was actually rather small for his age and embarrassed about it, said, "How do you do, Aunt Alice," and tried to pretend he had not heard.

Aunt Alice hugged and kissed Mr. and Mrs. Walker next and then fluttered over to Liz.

"So this is sweet little Elizabeth," she cried, "who writes such cute poetry! Your mother sent me one of your dear poems at Christmastime!"

This time it was Mrs. Walker who looked embarrassed because she knew that Liz did not like outsiders to read her poetry, and she had not told her that she had sent one to Aunt Alice.

Liz scowled and let Aunt Alice hug her, but she did not hug back.

The inside of the house was just as perfect as the outside. It was so perfect, in fact, that there hardly seemed to be a single place to sit that would not get dirty.

Mrs. Walker glanced hastily around at the white carpets and lemon-colored sofa cushions and then at the children who were mussed and grubby from long hours of travel.

"Wouldn't you two like to go outside and explore awhile?" she asked.

"This is a lovely neighborhood for children," Aunt Alice said. "My neighbors, the Bateses, have a boy just about Bruce's age."

"Do they live in the brown house?" Bruce asked with interest. He had noticed the house as they drove past it and had liked the way it was set off by itself and overgrown with trees and bushes. The grass at that house had not looked fake at all.

"Goodness, no!" Aunt Alice exclaimed. "That old place down by the end of the street? That eyesore has been up for sale for six months now and nobody even stops to look at it. No, the Bateses live right next door in that lovely big house with the garden. Jerry's very popular. There's always a group of boys playing over there."

The September sun was waiting for them when they went outside into the front yard. It fell warm across their heads and shoulders just as it had back in Albuquerque the day they had left. The sky curved rich and blue overhead, and there was a faint, far-off smell of autumn in the air.

"Elmwood, New Jersey, isn't really such a bad place," Bruce said. "That house down the street is groovy with those vines and bushes all over it, like a hide-out in the middle of a forest. I wish we were going to be living there."

"Well, we aren't," Liz said. She was not ready to see the good side of anything. "We're going to be living with allergic Aunt Alice and her white rugs, and I'm going to be 'sweet little Elizabeth' and you're going to be 'darling Bruce,' and I don't think I can stand it."

"Don't worry," Bruce said, "you won't be 'sweet Elizabeth' long. Not after she gets to know you. Besides, we'll be at school most of the time and Dad will be off at work. It will be Mother who has to sit in the house all day and soak it up."

His camera case hung by a strap from his shoulder. Now he opened it and took out his camera.

"Stand over there by the steps, and I'll get your picture. You can send it to Kim Caird to show to Bebe."

"All right," Liz said more agreeably. It was not often that Bruce offered to use his precious film to photograph his sister.

She had been standing by the porch steps for about thirty seconds when she heard Bruce say, "Hey!"

"Hey, what?" Liz asked him.

"Hey, look who's come visiting. He wants his picture taken. Look at him pose!"

Liz turned to find her brother aiming his camera not at her but at a big red dog who stood surveying them from the line between Aunt Alice's house and the one she had told them belonged to the Bateses.

"Where did he come from?" Liz asked, too surprised to be injured that she was no longer to be the subject of the picture.

"I don't know, but he shouldn't be out wandering. He's a beauty, isn't he?" Shifting his camera to his left hand, Bruce held the right one out to the dog. "Here, boy, come over and see me. Do you live around here?"

Waving his full red tail like a welcoming banner, the dog came eagerly forward to meet his new friend. Dropping to his knees, Bruce took the soft face in his hands and smiled into the brown eyes.

"I didn't think you cared about dogs very much," Liz said. "You never spend much time playing with Bebe."

"Bebe's a lap dog," Bruce said. "She doesn't want to play, she just wants to be petted. This big fellow's a man's dog. I bet he'd be fun to take —"

"What do you think you're doing with my dog?" The coldness of the voice cut like a knife through the soft afternoon.

Bruce glanced up in surprise at the tall, dark-

haired boy who was suddenly standing in front of him.

"Hi," he said in his friendly way. "You must be Jerry Bates. Aunt Alice said you lived next door. I'm Bruce Walker, and that's my sister, Liz. We're going to be your neighbors for a while."

"I didn't ask who you were," the boy said curtly. "I asked you what you think you're doing with Red Rover. That's an expensive dog, a pedigreed Irish setter. My dad gave him to me for my birthday, and nobody messes around with him without my permission."

"Bruce isn't hurting him. All he did was talk to him and take his picture." Liz left her place by the steps and came across the lawn to join the two boys. "I don't think this is your dog anyway. If he were he wouldn't be acting like that."

At the sound of the boy's voice, the dog had pressed himself tightly against Bruce's leg.

"He's mine, all right," Jerry Bates said. He snapped his fingers. "Come on, Red. Get over there in your own yard."

Instead of obeying, the dog dropped his head and whined nervously. He seemed to huddle even harder against Bruce, as though begging for protection.

"What's the matter with him?" Bruce asked. "I've never seen my sister's dog act like that. She just comes leaping when Liz calls her."

"He's stubborn," the tall boy said. "I haven't got him trained yet. Red Rover, you get over there, do you hear me?"

Raising his hand, he brought it down in a hard stroke between the dog's shoulder blades. Red Rover gave a yelp of pain. Dashing past his master, he ran across the yard and disappeared around the corner of the house.

"Is that what you call training?" Bruce gave a snort of disgust. "No wonder the poor thing's scared of you. He'll end up hating you before long if you keep treating him that way."

"You don't deserve to have a dog!" Liz's voice was choked with fury. "If I were Red Rover I'd jump up and bite your arm off!"

"He's got to learn to obey," Jerry Bates said. "You've got to show a dog who's boss. If he acts like he ought to, then I'm nice to him." He paused and then added in a pleasanter voice, "That goes for people too. You behave yourself, and maybe I'll let you come over sometime." He nodded at Bruce. "You, I mean. Your smart aleck sister is something else."

"What makes you think I'd come if you invited me?" Bruce asked. "Maybe I'd rather look for other friends."

"Sure, you'd come," Jerry said confidently. "All the guys in the neighborhood want to come to my place. I've got more stuff to play with than the rest of you put together. They're not going to risk getting in bad with me to be friends with a shrimp like you."

"My brother is not a shrimp!" Liz said angrily. "He's a straight-A student and a marvelous photographer! People always like Bruce! Back in Albuquerque he was the most popular boy in his class!"

"Maybe you westerners like shrimps," Jerry said. "Here in the East we eat them for dinner. We don't care much for fat little girls either, especially when they talk funny."

"I am *not* fat!" cried Liz, who really wasn't — only a little plump and not nearly as much that as she had been when she was younger. "And I don't talk funny! You're the one who sounds odd!"

"Ah doan' tawk funnnnnny!" Jerry gave an imitation of a western drawl like the ones on television programs. Then suddenly his eyes lifted and the sneering expression left his face. In its place there appeared the sweetest smile imaginable.

"Hi, Mrs. Collins!" he called. "How are you today?"

Bruce and Liz turned simultaneously to see Aunt Alice standing on the front porch with their parents close behind her. She was evidently bringing the Walkers out to show them her yard.

"Just fine, Jerry dear," she answered, her face breaking into a big smile at the sight of the three children together. "I'm so glad you've met each other! I was telling Bruce and Liz that we have the sweetest boy next door. I was coming out to introduce you, and here I see you're friends already!"

Chapter Two

To Liz the hardest part about starting a new school was the fact that Bruce was not starting it with her. For as long as she could remember, Liz had depended upon her brother to make friends for both of them.

Now in Elmwood, Bruce was a whole mile away at the Junior High School. It was a terrible, lonely feeling not to have him to lean on. Liz, who was never easy with strangers, found herself acting stiffer than ever.

Her first day at the new school a blond, bright-faced girl named Debbie Arquette had come up to her and asked if she wanted to play a game called pick-em-up. Liz, who had never heard of the game and was embarrassed to admit it, had said, "No, thank you."

"Oh, come on," Debbie said. "I'll show you how if you don't know."

"Of course, I know," Liz told her. "I just don't want to play, that's all."

Debbie had walked off, looking hurt, and Liz had been furious with herself, especially when she saw the little group of girls sitting under a tree tossing a ball in the air. Now that she saw what they were doing, she knew exactly what it was — the same game that she had played often in Albuquerque and called jacks. She had been very good at it last year and now, seeing the other girls playing, she was dying to rush over and say, "Oh, I do want to play after all."

When she thought about doing that, though, something knotted up inside her and she just couldn't. Instead, when Debbie or any of the other girls walked toward her, she looked through them as though she didn't see them at all.

Nobody ever asked her to play jacks again.

So, even though it was her own fault and she knew it, Liz found herself at the end of her first week in the Elmwood Elementary School without a single friend.

At home she pretended.

"We had such fun on the playground today," she told the family at dinner, or, "You should have heard the funny thing the girls were telling me at lunch!"

Then she felt terrible when Aunt Alice turned to her mother and said, "Oh, Betty, you are so lucky to have such a popular little daughter! Imagine making so many good friends so quickly in a new place!"

Actually, the thing Liz missed the most in the entire world was Bebe. Bebe had been her dog for almost three years now. She had gotten her for Christmas the year she was eight, when Bebe was just a puppy, so tiny that it had hardly seemed possible that she was real.

She had been under the tree in a box all wrapped with Christmas paper with little holes in the side so that air could get through. Liz had unwrapped the paper and felt the box move. Then the lid had popped off and there had been Bebe, pointed little face all bright and sparkling, nose wiggling, eyes shining, her tail long and thin like a piece of black wire thumping against the bottom of the box.

"We got Bruce a camera this Christmas, but we thought you would like this better," Mr. Walker had said, laughing at the startled look on his daughter's face.

Then, as though she had heard and understood the words, Bebe had jumped out of the box right into Liz's arms, and from then on there had been nobody else for either of them. Many people might like Bruce best, but not Bebe. Bebe thought there was nobody in the world as wonderful as Liz.

I wish she were here now, Liz thought as she left the classroom and walked down the long hallway to the outside door. All around her boys and girls rushed by with arms filled with books, laughing and chattering, calling to each other, "Wait! Wait for me!" It seemed to Liz that she was the only one in the whole school who had no friend to walk with when the final bell rang.

"I'll pretend Bebe is out there," she told herself. "I'll pretend she is waiting right outside the door."

The thought made her feel oddly better, and when she had walked out of the door and there was no little dog standing there, she told herself, "She's waiting on a little further, down by the street."

When she reached the street, she thought, "No — she didn't come this far. She's still at home at the corner of the yard, watching up the street, hoping I'll be coming."

Liz thought about Bebe all the way home. She thought about her so hard that she found herself getting more and more homesick. By the time she reached her own block her eyes were swimming in tears and she could hardly keep from sobbing out loud.

She hurried along the sidewalk, staring straight ahead of her — past the rows of maple trees, already beginning to redden with the chill of autumn nights, past the overgrown brown house with its FOR SALE sign out front, past a vacant lot and a yellow house with curtains over its windows, and turned up the neat white path which led to Aunt Alice's front door.

Then she stopped. She could not believe her eyes. There on the porch steps, sitting in a forlorn little heap as though he were waiting for someone, was a dog.

"Bebe?" Liz spoke softly, almost afraid that the sound of her voice would make the dog disappear. Wiping the tears from her eyes with the back of her hand, she crept up the walk until she was only a few feet away.

Now that she was close, she could see that the dog was not Bebe, was not even a bit like Bebe really, except for the color which was brown and the small size. This was a shaggy dog with long, dirty, uncombed hair hanging in all directions.

"Hi there, little dog," Liz said softly. "Are you waiting for me?"

The bundle of hair turned so that what seemed to be the front of the head was facing Liz, and from somewhere at the back of the bundle something began to twitch in what Liz thought must be a wag.

Reaching out, she pushed aside the hair that covered the dog's face and there, gazing soulfully up at her, were two bright button eyes.

"What are you doing, waiting here?" Liz asked. "Are you hungry? Come on, you poor little thing. Liz will get you something to eat." Gathering the dog up in her arms, she carried him through the house to the kitchen.

Her mother was there cutting up carrots. Mrs. Walker had fallen into the habit of doing the early part of the dinner when Aunt Alice was upstairs taking her afternoon nap and she could have the kitchen to herself.

"Oh, Liz, no!" she exclaimed, when she saw Liz standing in the doorway. "Take that dog right back outside!"

"But, Mother, he's hungry," Liz told her. "We can't let a sweet thing like this starve to death right on our front steps. Can't I give him a bowl of milk?"

"No, you can't," Mrs. Walker said firmly. "All you'd be doing would be encouraging him to stay. When you feed a stray animal you're just inviting it to make itself at home."

"Just a little milk, Mother?" Liz begged. "Please? Just think if this was Bebe, all hungry and nobody feeding her —" Her eyes began to get teary again at the thought.

"Well, he's not Bebe," Mrs. Walker said. "He probably has a perfectly good home around here and just wandered away from it. Now you take him back outside and give him a little shove to get him moving. Maybe he'll take himself home in time for dinner."

"He doesn't have a home," Liz said with certainty. "He doesn't have a collar or tag or anything, and he's so dirty and shabby and neglected —"

"Outside, Liz," Mrs. Walker said. "*Now*. Before Aunt Alice comes down from her nap and gets a sneezing spell. This is her home, dear, and we are guests. We have to abide by Aunt Alice's rules and fit into her way of doing things."

"Oh, all right," Liz said mournfully, and carried the dog outside.

"Poor baby," she murmured, rocking him back and forth in her arms. "Poor little unwanted thing!"

Glancing up the street to the left, she said, "There's

no sense sending you off in that direction. The people who own the yellow house are off on vacation or something, and then there's the vacant lot and the empty brown house. The other direction's worse." She gave a shudder as she turned to the right. "That horrid Bates boy lives there. He'd probably pull your legs off."

Looking across the street, she noticed a pleasant gray house with a swing set in the yard and bicycles parked in front.

"Maybe you'll find a home there," she said, trying to sound hopeful. "At least, it looks like your best chance."

Carrying the dog gently, she crossed the street and set him down in front of the gray house and gave him a little push in the direction of the porch. Then, quickly so that he would not follow her, she ran back across the street.

A new thought struck her just as she ran up the steps. "What if Bebe ran away! What if she ran away from the Cairds and set off to find me! What if she's out wandering now, just like that poor dog, with nobody to feed or care for her!"

It was such a dreadful thought that she felt sick to her stomach. Hurrying into the house, she rushed up the stairs to the room which was hers — it had been Aunt Alice's sewing room, but it had a couch in it which was made up like a bed — and flew inside and slammed the door.

On the table by the bed were a pencil and note paper. Snatching them up, Liz threw herself across the couch and began to compose a poem. "Bebe" was the title, and the words came pouring out, hurling themselves upon the paper:

> Weeping through the morning mists,
> I wandered all alone,
> Searching for the only thing
> That I could call my own . . .

Whenever she was upset, Liz wrote poetry and by now she had a large collection of poems. She wrote when she was happy too, and sometimes when she was bored, but those poems never seemed to turn out as well as the ones she wrote when she was miserable.

When her poems were completed, Liz copied them neatly onto clean paper and sent them off to *Good Housekeeping* and *Ladies' Home Journal*, which were magazines on her parents' coffee table at home. She had started doing this the year she was nine. She had heard somewhere once that Shakespeare had written his first play by the time he was eleven, and she had made up her mind that if she reached the age of eleven without having had a poem published she would give up writing and turn to something else.

Sometimes poems were hard to write and sometimes they were easy, but because she was already so worked up and filled with feelings, Liz found that this poem was the easiest she had ever written. Words came spilling over onto the page without her even having to think about them.

She was just finishing the last line when there was a rap on the door.

"Liz?" It was Bruce's voice. "Mother wants you to come down and set the table for dinner."

"Is it that time already?" Liz glanced up in astonishment to see dusk hanging heavy outside the window. "I didn't even know you were home."

Sliding the paper into her notebook, she got up and stretched. She felt good, as though all the unhappiness that had been inside her had drained off onto that sheet of paper. Tossing the notebook back onto the table, she left the room and went downstairs.

It began to rain as she set the table for dinner. It started as just a sprinkle, the lightest, slightest sound, like a gentle *tap-tap-tap* on the roof. By the time she had the napkins and silver on, however, the tapping had increased to a roar.

"I'd better check the upstairs windows," Bruce said, and went up to the second floor. "Dad's coming," he called down a moment later. "I can see his car coming down the street."

"I hope he took an umbrella with him," Mrs. Walker called from the kitchen, where she was helping Aunt Alice with the mashed potatoes.

The drum of the rain drowned out the sound of the car in the driveway, but they all heard Mr. Walker's feet as they thudded on the porch steps. Liz left the table and ran to open the door for him.

He came in dripping and shaking himself the way he would have into the brick hallway back home. Then he realized what he was doing and said, "Oh, my gosh — the rugs!"

"Oh, quick — newspapers! A bath mat! Bruce, run for some towels!" Aunt Alice came fluttering out of the kitchen to dab helplessly at the dampness on the snowy carpet with the corner of a dish towel.

Behind her father, Liz saw the water falling in a solid sheet as heavy and loud as a waterfall. Mr. Walker was shoving his wet hair back from his face. Bruce was rushing down the stairs, his arms laden with bath towels. Mrs. Walker was hurrying in from the kitchen with a roll of paper towels, her face creased with worry.

"Oh, dear," she was saying, "I hope they won't stain!"

They were all so occupied that there was one thing they did not see. Liz saw it, and she opened her mouth to speak. Then, slowly, she closed it again. I'm not going to say a word, she thought, as the little brown dog with the long wet hair came scampering in the door and between her father's feet and scurried down the hall and up the stairs.

Chapter Three

AT DINNER THAT NIGHT Liz could not keep her attention on what was going on at the table. Conversation drifted around her, hardly touching her ears.

The food on her plate sat there getting colder and colder until her mother said, "Liz, come down to earth, dear. Is something the matter? Don't you feel well?"

"Oh, no — no — I feel fine." Hurriedly Liz picked up her fork and began to eat. "I was just thinking."

Actually she had not been thinking at all, she had been listening. The smell of roast beef on the serving platter rolled out in warm, mouth-watering waves through the lower part of the house. How long would it be, she wondered, before the odor floated up the stairs to where a hungry dog was hiding? When it did, how long would he resist it?

She could almost hear the click of toenails on the stairs, as a bundle of wet hair came scurrying down to beg some supper.

Stay there, she willed silently. Stay there and wait a little longer. Liz will bring some dinner up to you soon.

As though she were reading her daughter's thoughts, Mrs. Walker said, "Liz is upset because she found a little stray dog this afternoon and I wouldn't let her bring it into the house. She is so used to having her own dog around to play with that it is a little hard for her to understand that it's just not possible here."

"Oh, mercy, no!" Aunt Alice raised her napkin to her face as though waving away the very thought of such a disaster. "I just can't, *can't*, get anywhere near animal hair! Even bird hair — I mean, feathers — I can't have them in the house either! All my pillows are foam rubber!"

"How about fish?" Bruce asked with interest. "Can you get near them?"

"I don't know," Aunt Alice admitted. "I've never been brave enough to try." She turned to Liz. "If you miss your pet so much, dear, why don't you go next door to play? Jerry has a dog. His parents just gave it to him."

"I don't think I'd like to play there," Liz said.

"Not like it at Jerry's!" Aunt Alice gave a little gasp of astonishment. "Why, you should see how his parents have fixed up the whole basement floor for Jerry and his friends! It's just beautiful — all pine paneled with Jerry's bedroom down there and a big game room with a Ping-Pong table and, goodness, I don't know what all. I can't understand why you children aren't over there playing every day!"

"Jerry and I don't hit it off," Bruce said shortly.

The statement was so out of character coming from Bruce that the adults at the table turned to stare at him.

"Why, son, that's not like you," Mr. Walker said. "You've never had any trouble making friends with other boys."

"I don't want Jerry Bates for a friend," Bruce said. "You should see the way he treats his poor dog."

"Oh, Bruce, I'm sure you're mistaken!" Aunt Alice exclaimed. "The Bateses are lovely people! I can't imagine that a boy like Jerry would mistreat a pet."

"You wouldn't think it to see him around grownups," Bruce said. "They always give him his way, and so he's real polite and nice. With his dog he's different. Red Rover's scared to death of him, isn't he, Liz?" He turned to his sister for support.

"What?" Liz had not heard the question. Stuffing the last forkful of food into her mouth she almost sighed aloud with relief. "Please," she asked, "may I be excused?"

"Not until the rest of us are finished," her mother said. "Then you can help Aunt Alice and me with the dishes."

Liz started to object, and then an idea occurred to her.

"I'll do the dishes by myself," she said. "You and Aunt Alice just rest. I'll clean up the kitchen too."

"Why, Liz!" Her mother looked stunned.

"Isn't that lovely!" Aunt Alice cried delightedly. "What a helpful little girl you are!"

Bruce, for his part, was staring as though she had gone crazy.

Liz had just finished stacking the last of the plates in the drying rack when her brother came into the kitchen. Closing the door behind him, he confronted her.

"Okay. Let's have it. What's the gimmick?"

"What do you mean, 'gimmick'?" Liz asked uneasily. "I just thought I'd save Mother and Aunt Alice some work and —"

"Come off it," Bruce said firmly. "Aunt Alice may think you're a 'helpful little girl,' but I know better. What's that you're hiding under your sweater? Come on, now —"

"Nothing," Liz insisted, trying to duck away from him, but he was too fast for her. He caught hold of the sweater and pulled it open.

"A dish of roast beef!"

"I — I thought —" Liz stumbled for an explanation. "I thought I might want a little bedtime snack."

"That's a fib and you know it!" Bruce could always

tell when she was lying. "What's the beef for? You'd better tell me."

"Oh, all right," Liz said reluctantly. "You'll have to promise, though, that you won't tell."

"Won't tell who?" Bruce asked.

"Anybody. Mother, Dad — especially Aunt Alice. This is a very deep secret. It's a matter of life and death."

"Okay, I promise." Bruce's curiosity could be contained no longer. "What is it?"

"I have a dog upstairs," Liz whispered.

"That stray Mother said you found? You brought it in after all?" There was grudging respect in Bruce's voice. "When did you manage to do that? Where do you have him?"

"I don't exactly know," Liz said. "He's someplace upstairs. He ran up right before dinner. I haven't had a chance to go up there. You should see him, Bruce, he's so pitiful — all wet and hungry with nobody to love him."

"Well, come on then," Bruce said. "Let's take the food up to him now while the family's all in the living room watching television."

Liz smiled at her brother gratefully. She was never certain how Bruce was going to react to things. Sometimes he was her closest friend, cooperating on anything she suggested, and other times he acted stuffy and self-righteous, almost like a grown-up.

This time, thank goodness, he was going to be all right.

"Let's go," she said, pulling her sweater over the plate again.

The noise from the living room drowned out the sound of their footsteps as they mounted the stairs. In the second-floor hallway Liz stopped and set down the dish of beef.

"Here, doggie!" she called softly. "Come here, dear! Liz has something nice for you!"

Only silence greeted her voice.

"That's funny," Bruce said. "If he's as hungry as you say, you'd think he'd come running. Dogs have good noses. They can tell when you have food."

"Maybe he's asleep," Liz said. "He's done a lot of running around today, poor thing, and he's probably exhausted. You start on this end, and I'll start on the other, and we'll find him."

Systematically, they began a search of the second floor. Bruce's area consisted of Aunt Alice's big bedroom and a storage closet and bathroom. Liz's included the guest room, which was now being used by their parents, and the sewing room. They met at last in the center of the hallway with blank faces.

"No sign of any dog that I can see," Bruce said. "I checked under beds and behind curtains and everything."

"He doesn't seem to be on this end of the hall."

Liz frowned. "Let's switch. I'll look through all the rooms you looked through, and you look through mine. One of us must have missed him."

"I'm sure *I* didn't," Bruce said, but he began a search of their parents' room while Liz started on Aunt Alice's.

She went through carefully, looking inside and behind things, crawling on her stomach to look under the bed, parting the curtains of the fluffy pink dressing table.

As she moved about she kept calling in a soft voice, "Here, doggie! Come out, little doggie!"

By the time she had gone through the bathroom, looking in the tub, in the dirty clothes basket, behind the commode, she was beginning to wonder if the dog was some kind of magician and had managed to vanish into thin air.

Bruce seemed to be feeling the same way. "Are you sure he's here?" he asked. "Maybe he ran down again when you weren't looking."

"I don't see how he could have," Liz told him. "From where I was sitting at the table, I could see down the hall to the foot of the stairs. Besides, if he'd come down it would have been straight into the dining room. That's where the food was."

"Well, he doesn't seem to be around now," Bruce said. "Maybe you daydreamed him. Maybe you just *wanted* to see a dog so much that you made yourself think you saw one."

"That's ridiculous," Liz said. This was the kind of grown-up comment Bruce sometimes made that made her want to hit him. "I didn't daydream anything. That dog is up here somewhere."

"I don't see how —" Bruce began, when their mother's voice rang from downstairs.

"Children? Have you had your baths yet?"

"No," they called back in unison.

"Then go ahead and take them. It's almost bedtime. I'll be up in a few minutes to tell you goodnight."

"Okay!" Bruce dropped his voice again. "I've done all the hunting I'm going to. I don't believe there *is* any dog. Dibs on the first bath."

"No, you don't, you took the first one last night." Liz picked up the plate of food from the floor and hurried to the sewing room.

Once inside she flicked on the light and got out her pajamas. Then she glanced around for a place to hide the dish. It would not do to have it sitting out when her mother came up to say good-night.

The door to the sewing closet on the far side of the room gaped open a crack. This closet was where Aunt Alice kept her patterns and materials. Crossing the room, Liz pulled the door wide and set the dish down on the top of a pile of patterns. She was just turning away when her eye was caught by a movement in the corner.

"So, there you are!" Liz dropped to her knees on

the closet floor. "No wonder we couldn't find you! You've got yourself hidden under a whole pile of material!"

Reaching over, she began to pull the cloth aside. "Why, you've made it into a kind of nest. What do you think you are, you silly thing, a bird? Don't you know that Aunt Alice is allergic to feathers just like dog hair and she —"

She stopped short. Then she caught her breath in a startled gasp. There in the soft bed she had made for herself was not only the shaggy brown dog, but three tiny brown-and-white puppies.

Chapter Four

"**I** DON'T CARE," Liz said, "you can't tell. You promised. You can't break a promise, Bruce Walker, no matter what."

"But, don't you see, I didn't know what I was promising! If I'd known, I wouldn't have promised."

Bruce regarded his sister with exasperation. Liz was the most interesting person he knew, even if she was part of his family. There were things wrong with her, to be sure, she was always shutting herself off someplace with her scribbling, and she had a bad temper, and sometimes she told lies. The thing was, though, she was never boring. Most of the boys he knew complained of their sisters' being drags. With Liz it was just the opposite; she never dragged. Sometimes, like now, Bruce almost wished she did.

"Look, sis," he said as patiently as he could, "you know as well as I do that we can't keep dogs here. The folks explained it to us before we ever left home, and you heard Aunt Alice at dinner tonight. All you have to do is mention the word *dog* and her nose starts dripping."

"I don't know why you're acting this way," Liz said. "You didn't start lecturing out in the kitchen. You said then that you'd help me find the dog and feed her."

"Well, sure, I wanted to feed her," Bruce said reasonably. "I wouldn't want any animal to starve. I could see letting her in out of a rain storm too. *Keeping* her here is something else. We can't do that. Besides, it's not just one dog now, it's four."

"What do you want to do, throw her out on the street?" Liz asked, trying to sound reasonable also. "With all those little puppies just an hour old? And the nights turning cold — and maybe more rain — and nothing to eat —"

"If we told Dad and Mother —" Bruce began.

"What could they do? You can't find homes for puppies who are this little, they have to stay with their mother. You know what the grown-ups would do. They'd say it was the only thing they could do. They'd send them to the pound."

"Well, gosh," Bruce said. This was something he had not thought about. He had gone with his parents to the pound in Albuquerque the day they got Bebe for Liz's Christmas present. He could still remember the cages of sad-faced animals, all waiting hopefully for somebody to want them.

"I'll tell you what," he said slowly. "We won't do

anything tonight. The dogs are all settled, and nobody has to know about them. In the morning, of course, there'll be a problem. After we leave for school Mother or Aunt Alice might come in here —"

"I won't go to school," Liz said. "I'll have a stomachache."

"I guess you could do that," Bruce agreed. "Mother always believes your stomachaches, and that way you could keep the door closed and say you wanted to sleep. That would give me a day to come up with some kind of plan. I hope I can do it in a day."

"Oh, I'm sure you can," Liz said confidently. She smiled, all the worry gone from her face.

Bruce himself was not nearly so certain. He stayed awake a long time that night thinking about the problem, and he concentrated on it so hard at school the next day that he missed three questions on his math paper. Arithmetic had always been easy for Bruce, and he was shocked when the teacher called out the grades.

From his seat in the next row, Jerry Bates turned and grinned. It was such a pleased grin that Bruce was more angry with himself than ever.

It had been an unpleasant surprise the first day of school to find Jerry in the class with him. It had been a shock for Jerry also.

"What are you doing here?" he had asked that first morning, when the two boys had found themselves side by side in the same homeroom. "You're not big enough for junior high."

"I was twelve in February," Bruce told him coldly.

"Nobody would guess it. You look like you ought to be back in grade school."

"Boys!" Miss Garwood had spoken from the front of the room.

At the sound of her voice, Jerry's expression changed completely. Glancing up quickly, he gave the teacher a warm, bright smile.

"I'm sorry, Miss Garwood. I was just trying to help our new boy feel at home."

"That was nice of you, Jerry." Miss Garwood's stern face softened. "You're very thoughtful, and I know Bruce appreciates it. Let's save our chatting for the playground and the lunch room, though. Okay?"

"Sure, Miss Garwood." Jerry dropped his eyes as though embarrassed. Under his lowered lids he shot Bruce a side glance.

"Save your chatting for the playground, shrimp, if you can find anybody to chat with," he whispered, as Miss Garwood turned her attention to a student on the other side of the room. "You're going to have a hard time finding any buddies in this class, I can tell you."

As days went by the statement had turned out to be more true than Bruce had expected. Jerry Bates *was* the leader of the neighborhood gang, which seemed to consist of most of the boys in the seventh grade. On the playground, it was Jerry who chose what games were to be played and told people which sides they were on, and it was Jerry who organized the after-school activities and conducted the special meetings in the basement of his house.

"What's with that guy?" Bruce asked Tim Kelly, who sat in front of him in history. "You fellows all jump when he speaks, like he was king or something."

"Nobody wants to make him mad, that's for sure. If he doesn't like you, he can make life pretty tough." Tim had a shock of red hair and the kind of open, freckled face that made Bruce wish he knew him better.

"Jerry is sort of like a king around here. He's an only kid, and his folks let him do anything he wants. He's got the whole basement floor of the house for his own. He can have all the guys he wants over there, and nobody ever bothers them." He laughed. "It's different at our place. I've got three little sisters. Nothing's private over there."

"I've got a sister too," Bruce said. "She gets on my nerves sometimes, but I'd sure rather have her around than Jerry Bates."

"Oh, he's not so bad as long as he isn't crossed up on things. He can be real charming and nice to the people he likes." Tim paused. "Of course, when things don't go his way, that's another story.

Like the kid who used to live in that house down the street from you, the one that's for sale now."

"What about him?" Bruce asked curiously. "What happened?"

"Oh, Jerry had some run-in with the kid. I don't know what it was about; it was before we moved here. Anyway, from the way I heard it, Jerry made life so miserable for him that the kid got where he wouldn't even go to school. Nobody would play with him or talk to him or anything for fear of getting Jerry mad at *him*. Finally, the family moved out. Before they left, though, the kid's dad went over and had a showdown with Mr. Bates and told him how rotten he thought Jerry was and how glad they were to be moving."

"Gosh!" It made Bruce feel good just to imagine the conversation. "What did Mr. Bates do?"

"Oh, nothing." Tim shrugged. "He didn't believe it. Grown-ups never see that side of Jerry. The Bateses think he's perfect. Anyway, Jerry got so mad when he found out about the kid's dad going over there that he went over to the house and threw rocks through all the back windows."

Bruce was appalled. "Why do you go around with him," he asked incredulously, "if he does that sort of thing? You trail him around on the playground just like the rest of them."

"Well, he's never done anything to me." Tim looked a little embarrassed. "We just moved to Elmwood last spring. All the fellows I met here were in Jerry's gang. When you're new in a place, you don't have much choice; you just join up with whoever's there. It's no fun being a loner."

"I'd rather be a loner than go around with somebody like Jerry Bates," Bruce said firmly.

There was a moment that afternoon, though, when he did not feel quite so definite. The last bell had rung and, as he left the building, Bruce saw a group of boys headed toward the park across the street. Tim was with them, and he was carrying a football.

As he reached the curb Tim glanced back and saw Bruce watching them. He smiled and waved and gestured for Bruce to join them. For a moment Bruce was tempted. He had not played football yet this season. He was small for his age, but he was fast, and when he got the ball he could usually leave the larger players behind him. It would be fun —

Then he glanced beyond Tim and saw the boy at the head of the group. Quickly he shook his head. No matter how much he wanted to play, he would not go crawling over to beg permission from Jerry Bates. Giving Tim a rueful smile, he turned on his heel and started off toward home.

The junior high school was closer to the house than the grade school that Liz attended, so in reality Bruce did not have very far to walk. It seemed a long way, however, when walked alone. Bruce was used to having friends, and the lack of them now was even harder for him than it was for Liz. She could shut herself off and write poetry and lose track of time, but Bruce had no such talent. For him the after-school hours dragged, endless with their emptiness.

Bruce walked slowly; there was nothing to hurry home for. When he came to the brown house with the FOR SALE sign he regarded it with interest.

I bet that kid was glad to move away from here, he thought sympathetically. I'll be glad myself when Dad finds out where he's going to be working.

He remembered Tim's statement about the back windows. Could Jerry really have been angry enough to break every one of them? It was hard to imagine, but then, there was no reason for Tim to have lied about it. Anyway, Tim did not look to be the sort of boy who lied.

He hesitated a moment and then, as his curiosity got the better of him, left the sidewalk and walked around to the far side of the house.

The moment he left the front yard, the bushes seemed to close in on him. They rose on all sides, untrimmed and untended, surrounding him like a jungle. The whole back yard was overgrown with grass knee-high and brambles and vines gone wild from neglect.

All the first-floor windows in the back of the house gaped empty, and piles of broken glass lay under them, glinting in the afternoon sunlight.

"What a mess!" Bruce regarded the destruction with disgust. "Somebody ought to report this to the police."

For one lovely moment he let himself toy with the idea of being the one to do it. It was a nice thought, and he enjoyed it before setting it aside for cold reality. He had no proof that Jerry was the one who had broken the windows. Tim himself had only heard it from other people. Jerry would deny it, of course, and look innocent, and give that wide, sweet smile that always melted grown-ups, and the police would not believe it, and certainly the Bateses wouldn't.

Discarding the idea regretfully, Bruce waded through the tall grass to inspect the damage more closely. Jerry had done a thorough job, all right. All that remained of the windows were some jagged slivers of glass that were still stuck in the frames.

Working with care so as not to cut himself on the sharp edges, Bruce began to remove these. They could be dangerous, he told himself. Some little kid might come around here and decide to crawl in to explore.

The windows were set low and would be easy to straddle. Looking in, Bruce could see an empty room with a door standing open to a hallway. Beyond that was another room with the door closed.

Dust lay thick over everything. How long had Aunt Alice said the house had stood empty? Six months, without anyone even coming to look at it?

It's too bad for a place to stay vacant like this, Bruce thought. There must be people in this world without a home who would be glad to look after the place just for a chance to sleep there.

It was then the idea came. It came suddenly like a great floodlight going on in his brain. It was the answer to everything.

For a moment he stood contemplating. Would it work? There would be plenty of problems. Still, even with problems, it seemed better than anything else they could come up with.

Tossing the last of the glass fragments into the bushes, he turned and began to run through the row of maples, across the vacant lot, toward Aunt Alice's neat white house down the street.

Chapter Five

IT WAS on a Friday afternoon that the dogs moved in.

"Thank goodness, it's Friday," Liz said. "This way I can spend all tomorrow over here getting them settled. Oh, Bruce, this is the most wonderful idea! Sadie and her puppies will think they're staying in a hotel!"

"Well, they had better not get too used to it," Bruce said. "As soon as the pups are old enough, we're going to find homes for every one of them and for Sadie too."

He spoke decisively to cover the fact that he was beginning to feel a little nervous. The idea had seemed so reasonable when it had first occurred to him: a vacant house with no one to tend it, four little dogs that needed a place to stay, so why not put them together for a few weeks?

The thing that was not reasonable was the way Liz was acting. In the day she had spent at home having her stomachache, she had formed a deep attachment for the group in the sewing closet. She had given them all names — Sadie for the mother and Tom, Dick, and Harry for the puppies — and she was acting as though she expected to be their mistress for the rest of her life.

"This is just an emergency thing, Liz," Bruce kept saying, as he followed her about from one empty room to another. "This is somebody else's property, even if they're not living here. We really shouldn't be using it at all."

"I know, I know." Liz's eyes were shining with excitement. "I think Sadie would like the pink bedroom at the front of the hotel, don't you? It's such a ladylike room, and that big window lets in so much light. We can fix her a bed in the corner, and when the puppies start walking they can go exploring down the hall to the living room."

"By the time they can do that, they'll be ready to leave," Bruce said. "We should start right now trying to line up homes for them. Does your school have a bulletin board? You could pin up a sort of announcement —"

But Liz was gone again, hurrying through to the kitchen to see if the faucets were working. It would be so much easier to fill Sadie's drinking bowl from there than to have to keep carrying water over from Aunt Alice's.

Liz was up at dawn the next morning and out of

the house before anyone else was awake. Mrs. Walker discovered her room empty when she went to call her to breakfast.

"I can't understand it," she said in bewilderment, as she joined the rest of the family in the dining room. "Liz never gets up early if she can help it. Where in the world could she have disappeared to?"

"Perhaps she's gone to someone's house," Mr. Walker suggested. "She talks as though she has plenty of school friends she likes to play with."

"This early?" Mrs. Walker shook her head. "Nobody goes visiting before breakfast." She turned to Bruce. "Did your sister say anything to you about having plans for this morning?"

"I — I don't think so. I mean, I don't exactly remember." Bruce felt his face growing hot. He had never been able to tell a lie successfully, even a little one.

"I do hope she doesn't stay out too long," Aunt Alice said. "Surely she knows that Saturday is cleaning day. There's just so much dust in the air these days that we have to keep ahead of it, don't we?" She gave a little sniff and reached for her handkerchief. "My poor nose! My allergies have been so bad these past few days. I can't imagine what's doing it."

By the time breakfast was over and Liz had still not returned, Mrs. Walker was looking really worried.

"Really, Bruce," she said, drawing him aside, "do you have any idea where Liz might have gone? It's so unlike her to miss a meal, and besides, she *does* know that Aunt Alice feels strongly about Saturday cleaning."

"We cleaned last Saturday and the Saturday before that," Bruce said. "For Pete's sake, Mother, we haven't had a chance to get anything dirty!"

"I know," Mrs. Walker said with a sigh, "but it must seem that way to Aunt Alice. She has lived alone so long that just normal tracking in and out brings in more dirt than she is used to. Besides, dust *does* seem to bother her terribly. The poor thing has been sneezing constantly."

"It's not the dust," Bruce said. "It's the —" He stopped himself. How could he possibly tell his mother, it's the dog hair and the dogs are gone now?

"Okay," he said reluctantly, "if Aunt Alice says it's cleaning day, I guess that's it. There's no reason Liz should be able to goof off when the rest of us can't. I'll go hunt her up."

Actually, Bruce was more irritated at Liz than his mother was. He knew exactly where she was and what she was doing, and he thought it a dirty trick for her to have run off on a Saturday and left him behind to answer questions.

As he left the house and started toward the hotel, he rehearsed under his breath the things he was going to say to her.

"Those dogs can get along by themselves until after we've got the chores done. If you start pulling this sort of stuff you're going to ruin everything. People are going to wonder what we're doing, and then we'll be in for it. Mother's already asking things —"

He was so intent on the speech he was planning that he was not aware of another presence until a voice called out to him, "Hey, shrimp, do you always go around talking to yourself?"

Turning with a start, he saw Jerry Bates standing only a few yards away from him. Three other boys were with him. One of these was Tim, who smiled and waved good-naturedly.

"Hi, Bruce! Where are you going in such a hurry?"

"Oh, just — well — my sister's wandered off some-place." Ignoring Jerry, Bruce responded to the pleas-anter greeting. "Mother asked me to go round her up."

"Like a cow on a ranch?" Jerry threw out the insult in a testing sort of way.

Bruce fought down the temptation to be drawn into a name-calling contest. Squaring his shoulders, he was about to walk on past when a flash of red caught his eye, and he saw Jerry's dog there with him. The dog was on a lead and had a rope tied across his chest. Alongside the boys on the sidewalk was a heavy wooden coaster wagon.

"What are you doing?" Bruce directed the question at Tim. "You're not going to harness Red Rover to that thing, are you?"

"Jerry wanted to try it," Tim said, "but it doesn't look as though he's going to get very far. Old Red has ideas of his own. He doesn't want to be a horse."

"I bet he doesn't," Bruce said. "That dog's not much more than a pup, even if he is a big one. His back's not strong enough to take the weight of that wagon."

"Look, shrimp," Jerry had dropped to his knees and was adjusting the poles that were attached to the sides of the wagon, "you run along and play with your sister. Nobody asked for your advice. We're getting along just fine without it."

"You are, huh?" Bruce tried to control the anger that was building up inside him. "You've got a beautiful dog there. What do you want to do, cripple him?"

Jerry finished knotting the poles to the rope harness. Then he got slowly to his feet. His face was dark with fury.

"Let's get something straight here. This is my dog — *mine!* He belongs to me, and I'll do what I want with him." He turned to the dog and snapped his fingers. "Up, Red! Let's see you go!"

The dog took a tentative step forward. The rope pulled tight against his chest, and he paused, bewildered. He was being ordered ahead and held

back at the same time. He was not certain what was expected of him.

"Bruce is right, Jerry," Tim said, as he saw the animal's confusion. "This is a game to you, but it isn't one to Red. Let's get him out of this tangle and play something else."

The other two boys, whom Bruce knew only from having seen them at school, had drawn off a few paces, reluctant to become involved in the argument. They were looking at each other uncomfortably, as though wishing they were somewhere else.

Jerry snapped his fingers again. "Get up, Red! Do you hear me?"

At the sound of his master's voice, the dog seemed to cringe and sank down to a crouch between the traces.

"You see?" Bruce said. "He won't even try. He's got sense enough to know he'll hurt himself."

"He'll try, all right, if he knows what's good for him. Come on, gang, help me get him going!" Jerry motioned to the watching boys. "You give him a shove while I get out in front and call him."

Bruce could stand it no longer.

"You leave him alone!" he shouted. "The poor thing's already scared sick! If anybody shoves him anyplace I'm calling my dad out here!"

"Oh, you are, huh?" Jerry's reaction was quick and violent. Catching Bruce by the shoulder, he gave him a hard shove backward.

Bruce's legs buckled as the edge of the wagon caught him at the back of the knees. An instant later all breath went out of him as his shoulders struck the floor of the wagon and his head hit the sharp wooden corner.

"Now, that's what our horse has been waiting for — a load to pull!" Jerry gave an excited laugh. "You stay right there, shrimp! You're going to get a ride you'll never forget!"

Raising the end of the leash high above his head, he brought it down with all his strength across the dog's lean haunches. Then, for good measure, he kicked as hard as he could at Red's left flank.

"Good gosh, Jerry!" Tim's face was a mask of horror. "What are you trying to do, kill him?"

Leaping forward, he grabbed for the leash, but the interference came too late. Red Rover let out a high-pitched, almost human scream of fear and pain and threw himself against the harness.

Bruce felt the wagon lurch beneath him and dazedly tried to pull himself to a sitting position. He was rolling along the sidewalk. The curbing loomed ahead. With all of his strength, Bruce threw himself over the edge of the wagon and onto the ground, just as the wagon crashed over the curb and into the street.

Free of Bruce's weight, the wagon seemed to fly forward against the dog's hind legs. This new assault was the final spur to the terrified animal. He plunged frantically out into the middle of the street, dragging the wagon behind him.

It was Tim who saw the car as it rounded the corner.

"Get him back!" he shouted, but by the time the words left his lips it was already too late. With a crash of splintering wood, the front wheel of the car struck the wagon and crushed it into the street.

Red Rover, the rope harness streaming behind him, tore free of the wreckage and kept running. A moment later the morning sunlight caught the sheen of his red coat at the end of the street, and then he was gone.

Chapter Six

SUNDAYS IN ELMWOOD were far from being Bruce's favorite days. Except that there was no cleaning to do, they were almost as bad as Saturdays.

It wasn't that he minded going to services. Church was something that had been part of Sunday for as far back as he could remember. It was just that back in Albuquerque church had been the beginning of the day, like an introduction. The whole family had gotten up early and gone and come home again with the rest of Sunday still ahead of them waiting to be used.

In Elmwood, church was the whole day and never seemed to be over. Aunt Alice liked to rise late, so breakfast never started until the middle of the morning. Then there was getting ready, which was terrible. Because there were so many of them in such a small amount of space, there just weren't enough closets and bureaus, and nobody could find anything exactly when it was needed.

"I'll sure be glad to get into our own place," Bruce grumbled, as he plowed through the pile of laundry stacked in the sewing-room closet. His own bed was the fold-down sofa in the den, and he was supposed to keep his clothes in the same chest of drawers as his sister.

"You've got those drawers so crammed with your writing junk there's no room for anything. Why don't you throw out some of those notebooks when you're through with them?"

"Those poems may be valuable someday," Liz said practically. "Think if Shakespeare had saved the things he wrote when he was ten."

"You can't compare yourself with Shakespeare," Bruce said. "He was a genius. He sold every single thing he wrote, and you can't sell a thing."

"I may sell something this week," Liz said pleasantly. "I mailed a poem to *Ladies' Home Journal* two whole weeks ago, and they haven't sent it back. Besides, how do you know that Shakespeare got everything published? He probably just didn't tell people when he didn't."

Liz was in an unusually sunny mood. She had slipped over to the hotel early that morning to give Sadie her breakfast and was anticipating another long visit with the puppies in the late afternoon. She had found both her gloves, which was something that seldom happened on Sundays, and there had been sweet rolls for breakfast, and it was quite possible that she might become a famous author with the arrival of tomorrow's mail.

In contrast with such cheeriness, Bruce's mood grew darker and darker. He could not find a clean shirt, and his good shoes were missing, and the resulting search took so much time that they were all late to services. Then it turned out to be Communion Sunday, which meant an extra half-hour, and Aunt Alice saw some friends afterward whom she had to stop and visit with. By the time they were home and at the dinner table, the whole day seemed to have dissolved with nothing to show for it.

Actually the Sunday irritations were only partly responsible for Bruce's depression. It had started yesterday with his battle with Jerry. Every time he thought back on the boy's cocky grin and his own undignified ride in the coaster wagon and the sight of the frightened dog cringing between the traces, anger rose within him until it nearly choked him.

"That guy shouldn't be allowed to own a pet," he had told Liz afterward. "You should have seen him after that car hit the wagon. Red Rover could have been killed, but that didn't worry him. He was just mad because his wagon was broken and the driver of the car wouldn't pay for it."

"He's the horridest person I know," Liz had agreed readily.

Still she had not been as upset as she should have been.

"How old are puppies when their eyes open?" she had asked a moment later, and Bruce had been disgusted. What use was a sister with a temper if she didn't lose it about things that were important?

Sunday dinner was finally reaching its end when the telephone rang. Aunt Alice rushed to answer it. A few moments later she returned to the table, shaking her white head regretfully.

"The saddest thing has happened," she said. "That was Mrs. Bates on the phone. She called to tell us that Jerry's dog is missing."

"That big red setter?" Mr. Walker looked up in surprise. "Why, I thought I saw the kids out playing with him today. Or maybe it was yesterday."

"They're afraid the dog may have been stolen," Aunt Alice said. "He's quite valuable, you know. Either that or he has run off somewhere. Children, do be sure and keep your eyes open for him when you're outside playing."

"If he has run off, he'll be back," Mr. Walker said. "When a pet gets hungry enough, he comes home."

"I hope he doesn't," Bruce said. "I hope he finds himself another home and never shows up around here again."

"Why, Bruce!" His mother turned to him in amazement. "What a thing to say!"

"I can't believe that of our Bruce." Aunt Alice gave a little gasp of shock. "Even if you and Jerry have had a spat, dear, you can't wish something like that. Why, think how heartbroken he must be!"

"If he is," Bruce said, "it's because he's lost something that belongs to him, not because he loves Red Rover. He's so used to having everything just the way he wants it that he's mad now because it isn't, that's all."

"Bruce, dear —" His mother caught his eye and raised her brows in a little that's-enough-for-now type expression.

"May I be excused, please?" Liz asked.

From her face, Bruce could tell that she had not been listening to any part of the conversation. Her whole mind was next door with Sadie and the puppies.

"Don't bother with clearing or anything," she said sweetly to her mother and Aunt Alice. "I'll do the clean-up."

"Why, Liz, that's three dinners in a row!" Aunt Alice beamed at her great-niece. "What a wonderful, helpful little girl you are! Your mother is so lucky to have such a helper in the family!"

"Yes, indeed," Mrs. Walker said doubtfully. Both her parents were looking at Liz in a funny way.

"I like to help," Liz said. "It's practice for when I'm grown and have my own kitchen." Hopping up from her chair, she began to carry out the dishes.

When Bruce came out to the kitchen a few minutes later, Liz was standing with her back toward him. When the door swung open, she bent over to conceal what she was doing.

"It's just me." Bruce let the door swing closed again. "What are you trying to do, make the whole family suspicious? All that 'I like to help' business. Couldn't you see Mother looking at you like she thought you were sick or something?"

"Well, it wasn't all a lie," Liz said defensively. "I *will* have a kitchen of my own someday. Of course, by that time I expect to be rich and famous enough to hire maids to take care of it."

"You'd better start wishing yourself rich now," Bruce said. "At least, rich enough to buy some dog food. You know you're not going to get away with this for long." He gestured toward the bowl of chicken and vegetables that his sister had been filling when he entered.

"I don't know about that. It's worked pretty well so far. Mother thinks Aunt Alice eats up the leftovers for a before-bed snack, and Aunt Alice thinks Dad does, and they're all too polite to say anything." Liz picked up the bowl from the counter. "I'm going to take this over to Sadie."

"Get the dishes done first," Bruce advised her. "Somebody might come out here to check on how you're doing."

"Really, Bruce, I'm just going to be a minute!"

Liz opened the door and, holding the bowl carefully so that the gravy would not spill, started out into the yard.

A moment later she was back.

"Bruce, he's out there!"

"Who?" Bruce regarded her blankly.

"Jerry Bates' dog! He's over in the corner of the

yard. He's dug a hole under a bush and he's lying in it, and he looks awful."

"Red's *here!*" Pushing past his sister, Bruce hurried out the door.

There was a dog, all right, under a bush as Liz had described. For a moment he could not believe that the dog was Red Rover.

Gone was the shiny coat, the proud lift of the head, the gaily waving plume of a tail. This dog's hair was dull and lusterless, matted with mud and burrs. His tail was curled under him, and his head was pressed against the ground. He did not lift it when Bruce approached or even when he spoke to him. A frayed rope circled his neck.

"It's the harness. He must have tried rubbing it off and got it pushed up around his neck." Bruce knelt on the ground and began to work with the knot. It was like a lump of steel beneath his fingers. The rope itself was so tight he could not get so much as a fingernail beneath it.

Liz, who had been watching in horror, ran back to the kitchen. When she returned she was carrying a paring knife.

"Will this help? Maybe you can cut it."

"I hope I can without cutting Red." Bruce took the knife and began sawing nervously against the thinnest part of the rope.

The dog slumped beside him, too miserable to care what was being done to him. When the rope gave way at last, he drew a long rasping breath and looked up gratefully into Bruce's face, but still he did not try to move.

"He could have strangled." Bruce ran his fingers gently along the dog's throat. There was a raw, hairless circle where the rope had cut into the tender skin. "He couldn't have lived that way much longer. If you hadn't found him and we hadn't gotten that rope off when we did, he would have died."

"Right next door to his own house!" Liz's voice was low and shaken. "He'd rather dig a hole and die in it than go back home to Jerry! Oh, Bruce, imagine how scared he must be of him if he would do that!"

"Don't worry, old fellow." Bruce caressed the drooping head. "I'll take care of you. Nobody's ever going to hurt you again."

"But, if we take him back —" Liz began.

"We're not going to," Bruce said quietly. "We've got a new tenant for our hotel."

Chapter Seven

GETTING RED ROVER to follow them was not difficult. The big dog seemed to realize that Bruce was his new master. All he had to say was, "Come, Red," and the poor animal struggled to his feet and allowed himself to be led through the back yard of the house next door and across the vacant lot to the dog hotel. The problem came with getting him through the window.

"We'll never make it," Liz said, studying the distance from the ground to the sill and then turning to study the size of the dog. "He's too heavy to lift that far. Do you suppose we could get him to jump?"

"Not in the condition he's in now," Bruce said. "The poor fellow can hardly even walk. We'll have to try lifting him. There's no other way."

A voice spoke from behind them. "Why don't you rig a ramp?"

Bruce froze. Then he turned slowly to face the speaker. His face was pale.

"What are you doing here?" he asked in a low, tight voice.

Tim Kelly regarded him calmly.

"Looking for you. I saw you crossing the lot, but I couldn't catch up with you."

He paused and then repeated his original statement. "You could put up a ramp. We've got some old lumber over at our place if you want to use that. All it would take would be a couple of boards propped against the sill."

"You're a spy!" Liz burst out furiously. "I've seen you with Jerry! You're one of his gang, and you're going to run back and tell him we have Red Rover."

"Don't be a goon," Tim said. "If I were going to do that, would I be offering you boards for a ramp?"

"Look, what's the deal?" A little color was beginning to come back into Bruce's face. "Why do you want to help us hide Red?"

"Do you think I want Jerry to get another crack at him?" Tim asked. "I was in on that scene yesterday, remember? What do you think I am, some kind of monster? I wouldn't send any animal back to that."

"I thought you wanted to be part of the gang, though," Bruce said. "You don't want to be a loner, do you? You told me you didn't."

"I wouldn't have to be, would I?" Tim said slowly. "I mean — well, one friend, the right kind of friend, is worth more than being part of a mob of guys following along behind somebody like Jerry. Anyway, that's the way it's beginning to seem to me." His blue eyes were questioning. "How about you?"

Bruce nodded soberly, but inside he felt like cheering. "It's *always* seemed like that to me," he said.

The boys stood silent a moment, a little embarrassed by the sudden change in their relationship. Then Tim grinned. "Okay, that's settled. Now, how about going over to my place and getting the boards?"

"Wait a minute," Liz broke in cautiously. "Before you can be part of the hotel, you've got to promise on your honor that you won't tell anybody. Not just about Red, but about Sadie too. And Tom and Dick and Harry."

"Tom, Dick, and Harry?" Tim looked bewildered. "Who are they? Who's Sadie?"

"They're the rest of the dogs," Liz explained. "They have the pink bedroom. I think we should give Red the den for his room. That way he'll have more space to move around in when he starts feeling better."

"You mean you've got four dogs in there already!" Tim exclaimed incredulously.

"You have to promise," Liz persisted.

"For Pete's sake, of course he promises," Bruce said. "Now, you stay here, sis, and keep an eye on Red while Tim and I get the stuff for the ramp."

Tim's house turned out to be the gray one across the street from Aunt Alice's with the front yard full of swings and bicycles. The lumber he had spoken about was stacked along the side of the house.

As they selected the boards they would need, Bruce noticed several round, freckled faces, much like Tim's, gazing down at them from an upstairs window.

"Those are my sisters," Tim said. "I told you how nothing over here is ever private. They'll think we're taking the boards over to Jerry's. He's been talking about wanting to use them to build a clubhouse."

"Well, Jerry will know that's not where we're taking them," Bruce said, glacing worriedly in the direction of the Bates house. There was no way to get the boards across the street except to carry them openly. Although no one was in evidence, he could not help the uncomfortable feeling that Jerry was somewhere peering at them. "Which is his window?"

"It's the ground window," Tim said, "on the side facing your aunt's house. That's where he has his bedroom. Actually the whole basement floor is his. He's got a Ping-Pong table and a kind of gym set up for working out. All he has to do is ask for something and his folks run and get it for him."

"Let's carry the boards down the driveway into our back yard," Bruce suggested. "That way, if Jerry's watching he'll think we're going to build something back there. Then we can cut over through the yard next door and across the lot to the hotel."

As they were crossing the yard, Mrs. Walker opened the back door and called out to them.

"Bruce, do you know where your sister is?"

"She's — well, she's right around here," Bruce said awkwardly. "I just saw her a minute ago."

"I want you to find her and send her home right now," his mother said in an exasperated voice. "She said she would do the kitchen, and she hasn't even rinsed off the plates yet! Aunt Alice gets terribly upset when things are left a mess."

Liz was sitting in the grass in the yard behind the hotel. She had Red Rover's head in her lap and was gently stroking his ears.

"You don't have to tell me — I heard her," she said, when Bruce and Tim came up to her. "My, she was yelling! Mother never used to yell that way."

"You'd better get over there," Bruce said. "You did say you'd do the clean-up."

"I didn't say when I'd do it," Liz said. "At home Mother never minded if we let the dishes sit awhile before we washed them. Why should it matter so much here?"

"Because it does, that's all." Bruce lowered his end of the boards to the ground. "How do you want to do this, Tim?"

"Simple." Tim lifted the ends he was holding and leaned them against the window ledge. Side by side, they became a slanted bridge between the window and the ground. "Now comes the tough part — getting Red to walk up it."

"I'll go in and call him," Bruce said.

"That won't work. He doesn't come when he's

called. I've seen Jerry call him lots of times and he just cowers and pretends he doesn't hear."

"He'll come to *me*," Bruce said with certainty.

Walking to the top of the ramp, he turned to face the dog. "Here, Red!" he called softly. "Come up here with me!"

Without an instant's hesitation, Red Rover lifted his head from Liz's lap and got stiffly to his feet. Crossing to the ramp, he went slowly up it until he reached Bruce.

"You see!" Bruce's voice was triumphant as he gently eased the big dog through the window. A moment later they were both inside the house.

"He's picked you for his master, that's for sure," Tim said respectfully, when he and Liz had joined Bruce inside. He glanced about with interest. "Where are the rest of your tenants?"

"In the front bedroom." Liz darted ahead to lead the way down the hall. "Sadie just loves it. It's so sunny and pretty. Of course, Red is a man's dog — he'll like the den. It's all wood paneled."

Sadie's room, when the door was thrown open, was as much of a surprise to Bruce as it was to Tim. He had not been in it himself since they had settled the dogs in on Friday, and though he knew that Liz had been spending all her time there, he had not guessed the extent of her activities.

The room shone! Gone were the dust and the cobwebs which had collected during the long period that the house had stood empty. For a girl who did not like housework, Liz had swept and scrubbed until the floor and woodwork gleamed. The glass of the windows had been cleaned so that the sunlight flooded through, bringing the pink-papered walls to vibrant life.

But this was not all. A pink throw rug lay across the bare boards of the floor. Pink rosebud curtains hung at the side windows. A bed, fashioned from a clothes basket, stood at the corner of the room, and inside it Sadie and her puppies lay, curled in luxurious comfort, upon the palest and softest rose-colored sheets.

"Good gosh!" Bruce stood staring in amazement. "Where did you get all the stuff to do this?"

"Different places." Liz looked smug. "I found the rug up in Aunt Alice's attic. It was just lying up there, all rolled up in a corner. The basket was down in the basement. It had old magazines in it."

"But the sheets and the curtains!" Bruce stepped closer to examine them more critically. "This isn't old cast-off stuff. This is brand-new material!"

"Nobody was using it." Liz began to look uncomfortable. "It was in the sewing closet."

"Then Aunt Alice must have bought it for something," Bruce said. "That's stealing, Liz! You can't take material that someone has paid good money for and cut it up for fun!"

"It wasn't for fun," Liz said. "It was for Sadie.

She's a new mother. She needs to have pretty things around her. Besides, Aunt Alice was never going to make anything out of that. I'm sure she wasn't. She hasn't sewed a single thing since we've been living with her."

"How could she when you're sleeping in the sewing room?" Bruce reminded her. "It can't be the greatest thing for the old lady, having a family land on top of her like this. Maybe she's just counting the days until she can have her house to herself again and sew like crazy."

"Oh, I don't think so," Liz said decidedly. "I bet she got that material on sale without having any use for it. She's probably been looking at it ever since, just wishing it wasn't there."

"Why did you use it on just one window?" Tim asked with interest.

"Because that window is on the side of the house where the bushes are. If I'd done the front one, people could have seen them from the street." Liz turned pleadingly to her brother. "You do think they look nice, don't you, Bruce?"

"It's not a question of whether they look nice," Bruce said. "The thing is, you've cut up something that doesn't belong to you. You're going to have to replace that material, Liz. You can't just *take* things, even for Sadie."

"You took Red," Liz muttered. "That's stealing

too, isn't it? I bet a dog like Red Rover costs a lot more than some old cloth."

"That's different," Bruce said defensively. "I took Red for his own sake."

He paused as the logical part of his mind fought with his feelings. Red Rover was a valuable dog, of that there was no question. Mr. Bates had undoubtedly paid a good price for him when he bought him for Jerry.

"I'll pay them," he said now, after a long moment of consideration. "I'll find out how much a good Irish setter costs, and I'll save up the money and pay it. I'll leave it in an envelope in the Bateses' mailbox."

"It looks like this hotel is getting to be an expensive operation," Tim remarked. "What about food? How are you paying for that?"

"I've been taking table scraps," Liz said. "Bruce thinks that won't work much longer."

"It certainly won't after today," Bruce said. "Not after the way you ran out on cleaning the kitchen. From now on you're going to have Mother or Aunt Alice standing over you every time you pick up a dishcloth."

"I've seen how Red Rover eats," Tim said. "You'll never take care of him with table scraps. It's going to have to be dog food and plenty of it. I guess we'll just have to go to work and start earning."

"We?" Bruce said. "Look, Tim, you aren't responsible. It's Liz and I who have got ourselves into the hotel business."

"Well, I'd like to be a partner," Tim said. "That is, if you want me. I've never had a dog of my own. This way I can be part owner of five of them!"

Chapter Eight

HAVING TIM KELLY part of the hotel staff was nice for Bruce, but it took Liz only a short time to discover that she did not like it at all.

"I wish he had never stuck his nose in," she grumbled.

"You're nuts," Bruce told her. "Tim is a great guy. Look how he's helping us! We could never have managed to keep Red in dog food if Tim hadn't found us after-school jobs."

"Sadie doesn't like him," Liz said. "She knows that he isn't used to dogs. It upsets her to have him tramping in to look at the puppies."

This was completely untrue, and both of them knew it. Sadie was a proud mother and delighted to show off her puppies to anyone, including Red Rover. The thing that Liz really resented was the fact that she was no longer able to run things the way she wanted. Until now, she and Bruce had been equal partners, with Liz actually holding the position of manager.

Now suddenly everything seemed to have gone out of her hands.

"Tim and I are earning the money to run this place," Bruce said. "It's up to us to decide what we're going to do with it."

The two boys were working every afternoon and on Saturdays raking yards around the neighborhood. Out of their earnings they had purchased a whole case of dog food and a brush and comb for Red and some salve for the injured area around his neck. The rest of the money they were setting aside in a special fund to be used for the purchase of Red Rover.

"You might spend some of it on Sadie," Liz said angrily. "There are so many things she needs — her own brush, for instance, and a collar and a cushion for her bed and balls and rubber bones and things for the puppies."

"Sadie ought to feel lucky just to be getting some of Red's dog food," Bruce said. "Remember, you've still got to pay Aunt Alice for the material you took. You haven't put aside any money for that, not even your allowance."

"I couldn't," Liz said, bristling. "I borrowed against it last month to buy a book, and then there was a movie — no, two movies — that I *had* to see, they might never have come back again. And the laces in my sneakers broke, and I spilled Mother's nail polish, so I had to buy another bottle of *that* —"

"That's okay," Tim said soothingly. "Girls don't

know anything about earning money. My sisters never earned a dime in their lives."

The superior tone of his voice infuriated Liz even more than Bruce's statements, and the worst of it was that she could not think of a thing to answer. It was true that she had never earned money, and with her mother irritated at her and Aunt Alice no longer so certain that she was a "dear, helpful little girl," it did not look as though she was going to be offered many opportunities to do so.

"I'm reaching the end of my patience with you, Liz," Mrs. Walker had told her in the firmest voice Liz had ever heard her mother use. "Back in Albuquerque we lived in a very casual way, but here we are living in somebody else's home. It's hard when there are so many people in a small house, and you will have to do your share to help."

"Aunt Alice is a picky old maid," Liz said irritably. "All she thinks about is dust, dust, dust. She's boring and gushy and I wish we were living in a hotel."

"She is not an old maid," Mrs. Walker said. "She was married many happy years to your father's Uncle Peter. If she seems 'gushy' with you, it's simply that she isn't used to children. She never had any of her own, and she doesn't really know how to talk to them."

"What's so hard about talking to children?" Liz asked. "Children are human beings."

"So are grown-ups," her mother said quietly. "If

you were to open that stubborn mind of yours a little, my dear, you might let yourself discover it. Very few people are boring when you really get to know them."

Liz opened her mouth to answer and then, at the look on her mother's face, she closed it again. Mrs. Walker was no longer reaching the end of her patience — she had already reached it.

Aside from the fact that she was at odds with almost everyone in her family, Liz had another reason for being cross and irritable; her poem had come back from *Ladies' Home Journal*. She had been very hopeful about that poem. It had been called "Death Owns a Ship" and was the most dramatic thing she had ever written, and the magazine had kept it for three whole weeks.

Toward the end of that time she had become quite certain that they had decided to buy it and were trying to make up their minds how much to pay her. Every day she had rushed home from school to see if her check had arrived, and she had had great dreams of strolling casually along the sidewalk past the yards where Bruce and Tim were working, with Sadie and the puppies marching before her, each with a diamond-studded leash attached to an emerald-studded collar.

It had been a terrible disappointment to walk into the house one day and find an envelope waiting for her on the hall table with her poem inside and a little note saying, "We're sorry we can't use this, but do try us again when you are older."

Older, Liz thought! She would be eleven the first day of December. That was less than two months away.

"What's the matter, Liz?" her father had asked her at dinner that night. "You're so quiet. You must be off in space somewhere composing a new poem."

Liz drew a long breath and made her announcement. "No," she said. "I'm not. I've decided I'm not meant to be a famous writer. In fact, I'm never ever going to write a poem again."

There was a moment of complete silence. Everyone at the table turned to stare at Liz in astonishment. Even Aunt Alice stopped talking with her mouth still half open.

"Why, Liz," Mrs. Walker said finally, "you've been so sure you wanted to be a writer! You've been writing for over two years now. How can you simply decide to stop?"

"I've changed my mind," Liz said. She did not want to talk about it any further because she was afraid she might begin to cry. She had been so certain that she would become famous within the time limit that she had set for herself. "I'm going to be something more interesting like a — a — a lady flyer or a ballet dancer."

"You're not graceful enough to be a dancer,"

Bruce said. "You can't be a flyer either because you can't stand heights. You won't even look at the slides I took of the Grand Canyon because they make you dizzy."

"Then I'll be a schoolteacher," snapped Liz, blinking back her tears.

The thought of prickly Liz patiently teaching school was so incredible that no one could think of a single comment, and the rest of the meal took place at a very quiet table.

The next day at school the subject came up all over again. This time it came from Miss Crosno, Liz's teacher.

"Who was it," she asked, "who turned in a poem along with the English compositions this week? There isn't any name on it, and I don't recognize the handwriting." When no one in the class raised a hand, she continued, "It's called 'Bebe.' It's about a child who loses her dog."

"Oh!" Liz was so startled that she spoke out before she could stop herself. "That's mine, but I didn't mean to turn it in. I guess I just got an extra paper mixed in with the composition sheets in the notebook."

"I'm glad it was turned in," Miss Crosno said. "It's a very nice poem with a great deal of feeling. Would you like to come up front, Liz, and read it to the class?"

"No, thank you," Liz said.

Then, because this sounded rude even to her own

ears and, after all, Miss Crosno would be the one who would be making out report cards in another two weeks, she added, "I never read my poems to anybody but the family. If they're not good enough to be published, they're not good enough for people to have to listen to."

"Do you submit your poems to magazines?" Miss Crosno asked. "Which ones do you send them to?"

"To the ones on Mother's coffee table," Liz said. "But I don't any longer. I've done it for two years now and used up about a million stamps, and it hasn't gotten me anywhere, and I think that's enough."

That day at lunchtime, when Liz was unloading her tray at the corner table in the cafeteria where she usually sat and read, she was surprised to find another tray placed suddenly beside her own.

"May I sit here?" Debbie Arquette asked her.

Debbie had not tried to speak to her since the time she had asked her to play jacks in the school yard. Liz could not imagine why she was bothering to do so now.

"I don't care," she said. "Sit wherever you want to."

Debbie was unloading her tray and did not seem to notice the ungraciousness.

"I had to talk to you," she said, "after this morning and what Miss Crosno said about your poem. Before I thought you were just unfriendly, but I

didn't know then that you were a poet. That makes
it different. I mean, lots of poets don't play jacks
and things."

"I do play jacks," Liz said. "I didn't know that's
what you meant by pick-em-up."

"Why didn't you say so then?" Debbie took the
seat opposite and regarded her solemnly out of wide
blue eyes. "The thing I wanted to tell you is — now
don't repeat this to anybody, I don't want the other
kids to think I'm peculiar — but I write poetry too."

"You do!" Liz said. It had never occurred to her that other girls ever wrote poetry.

"I have a whole notebook full of poems at home," Debbie said. "I keep it hidden under my bed so my brother won't see it. He says only oddballs write poetry."

"That's not so," Liz said. "It takes very bright people to be poets. Think of Shakespeare and people like that! Besides, you're not an oddball. You're very popular."

"Yes," Debbie admitted, "I guess I am. Still, I don't have anybody I can talk to — I mean *really* talk to — about things that matter. Most of my friends feel just like my brother does. You don't want people to think you're strange."

"I don't mind it," Liz said. Then she paused and added more honestly, "Well, yes, I do mind it some. It would be nice to be very popular. Maybe I will be now that I've stopped writing."

"What do you write about?" Debbie asked. "I mean, what *did* you write about back when you were a poet?"

"Sad things mostly," Liz said. "My last poem, the one I sent to the *Journal*, was about shipwrecks." She drew a deep breath and quoted:

"Death owns a ship that roams the seas,
  A ship that the boldest seamen dread.
  It's made of the air and the clouds and the storm,
  And its cargo is the dead."

"Goodness!" Debbie's blue eyes widened admiringly and she gave a shudder. "That's the goriest thing I've ever heard, Liz! I don't see how any magazine could help but buy it!"

"Well, they didn't," Liz said. "I'm practically eleven now, and I can't be spending all my time on something that isn't bringing any success. Especially now when I've got to start finding ways to earn money the way Bruce is, because Sadie isn't getting half the nice things that Red Rover is getting and —"

She stopped herself in horror and clamped her mouth closed tight.

"Who is Sadie?" Debbie asked with interest, exactly as Tim had the first day he came to the hotel.

Perhaps it was the thought of Tim's question that did it, Tim's question and the memory of Bruce's answer, "Of course, he won't tell." What right had Bruce had to decide whether or not Tim was to be trusted when she herself had not decided? Why should Bruce be able to pick out a friend and bring him in and make him a member of the hotel staff when she, Liz, didn't?

Two boys and one girl — it wasn't a fair balance. How could the girl ever hope to have anything her way as long as the boys outnumbered her? But if there were *two* girls —

Thoughtfully, Liz regarded the girl across the table. Debbie was certainly not a blabbermouth. If she had been, she would never have kept secret for so long the fact that she was a poet.

"Can you keep a secret?" Liz asked.

"Of course." Debbie's voice dropped to a whisper and she leaned forward eagerly. "Is it about a poem?"

"No," Liz said. "It's Sadie. She's a dog, and Red Rover's a dog, and there are three others who are just puppies. My brother and I are running a hotel for them."

"A hotel!" Debbie exclaimed. "You mean you take homeless dogs in off the streets and give them a place to stay?"

"Something like that," Liz said.

Debbie's face was aglow with excitement. "How fabulous! Do you suppose — oh, Liz, does the hotel have an extra room for another guest?"

"It has all sorts of rooms," Liz said. "There's a whole second floor. But what other guest are you thinking about?"

"MacTavish," said Debbie.

"Who?" Now it was Liz's turn to look blank.

"Don't you know him? It's that little gray terrier who always hangs around the school grounds. He used to belong to a boy who went to school here, but last summer the boy's family moved away and they didn't take MacTavish with them."

Liz was horrified. "You mean they just left him here to starve?"

"Oh, he doesn't starve," Debbie said. "All the

kids feed him, and he sits outside the cafeteria at lunchtime and the ladies who do the cooking put out scraps for him. The thing is, it's starting to get cold now. What will he do when winter comes and he doesn't have any warm place to go?"

"Isn't there anybody who wants him?" Liz asked. She thought of the careful plans her own family had made to leave Bebe at the Cairds' when they had been forced to leave her in the West. How could anyone possibly get into a car and drive off without making any kind of arrangements to have their pet cared for?

"Couldn't *you* take him?" she asked.

"I'd love to," Debbie said, "but my mother has a cat. Fluffy is a very special, blue-ribbon Persian, and she hates dogs. If we got one, Mom is afraid she might run away."

"Isn't there anyone else who might want him?"

Liz asked the question, but her mind was flying ahead of her. It was moving on wings down the hallway that led from Sadie's pink bedroom, past the paneled den where Red Rover stayed, up the stairs to the second-floor hall where a whole row of doors opened into unused bedrooms.

I wonder, she thought, if a gray dog would like blue wallpaper better than green?

Chapter Nine

THERE WAS NOTHING difficult about locating Mac-Tavish. When school was out for the day, Debbie led the way to the back of the cafeteria, and there he was. When she saw him, Liz had the immediate feeling that he was waiting there just for her.

"I wish I could help you get him to the hotel," Debbie said. "I would if I didn't have a Scout meeting."

"I can manage fine," Liz told her. "He isn't so big. I was afraid he might be the size of Red Rover."

Actually, although he was a small dog, MacTavish was large for carrying, for he had gained a good deal of weight eating sandwich crusts and spaghetti left over from the cafeteria meals. Liz was panting by the time she got him to the hotel.

Still, it was worth it! Never had she seen a dog so happy! She had decided to give him the blue room, as it had a built-in window seat from which a dog could look out over the back yard, and Mac-

Tavish leaped up there at once. From there he jumped to the floor and ran about sniffing, exploring the room from one corner to another. Then he leaped upon Liz. Wagging and licking and wriggling with delight, he burrowed into her arms, making little squeaking sounds of joy.

Hooray! he seemed to be saying. At last I have a home!

"You poor thing! Imagine your master going off and leaving you!" Liz hugged the dog hard, ducking her head to keep the busy pink tongue from washing her face. "Thank goodness, Debbie told me! Just wait until Bruce sees you! Sadie's so busy with her puppies, she isn't much company for Red Rover. Bruce will be so glad to have a friend for Red to play with!"

In this she was mistaken. Bruce was not happy at all.

"Another dog!" He regarded his sister with disbelief. "Liz Walker, you must be crazy! Tim and I are working ourselves to death to take care of the ones we already have!"

"He won't eat much," Liz said. "He's already fat from all the starches he got at school. He needs to reduce. One meal a day should do him just fine."

"Fat dogs eat more than thin ones," Tim volunteered. He and Bruce had stopped by the hotel on their way over to the Kellys' to get their rakes. "It's the same with fat people. Their stomachs

stretch, and it keeps taking more and more food
to fill them up."

"That's not so," Liz contradicted. "Aunt Alice is
fat, and she hardly eats anything. Besides, we won't
have to buy all the food. Debbie thinks if we ask
the ladies at the cafeteria to save the scraps and
put them in a bag —"

"Debbie!" Bruce pounced upon the unfamiliar
name. "Who's Debbie? Have you been blabbing
around about the hotel? I thought we all promised —"

"I haven't been blabbing," Liz said. "I only told Debbie. She's my best friend, just the way Tim is yours."

"What do you mean, your best friend?" Bruce exploded. "I've never even heard of her! If you have a best friend, why haven't you ever had her over?"

"I am going to have her over," Liz told him, "tomorrow. She's going to help me with the hotel housework. Now that we have six guests, there's really too much work for one person to do alone. You boys never help."

"Never help!" Bruce was so angry it was all he could do to keep from grabbing his sister and shaking her until her teeth rattled. "What do you call all those hours Tim and I put in after school and on weekends raking leaves all over the neighborhood?"

"That's not the same thing," Liz said. "It really isn't, Bruce. Not at all."

Then, because it seemed very likely that her brother might be going to hit her, she snatched MacTavish into her arms and ran out of the room.

"You shouldn't let her get to you like that," Tim remarked later, as the boys collected their rakes from the Kelly garage. "She's just acting like a girl. My sisters are the same way sometimes."

"I know," Bruce said wearily. "I never used to get so mad at her. It's just today. Bringing home that darned dog without even checking with us first —"

"He seems like a nice dog," Tim said. "I've always kind of liked terriers. Those pups of Sadie's are going to be ready to leave home in another week or so anyway."

"That's true. They're already beginning to eat solid food." Bruce brightened slightly. "That will cut things down by half."

Even so, he had far from a joyful expression on his face as he and Tim set off down the street toward their afternoon job.

The truth of it was, Bruce was exhausted. He had always been a boy who enjoyed having time to himself — time for reading, for playing with other boys, for puttering around with his photography. Now suddenly there was no time at all. When he was not at school he was working, and when he wasn't working he was trying to study; *trying* because by the time dinner was over and he was ready to settle down to his books, he was usually so sleepy that he could not keep the words on the page from running together.

It showed on his grades.

"Bruce, I don't understand what's happened," Mr. Walker said the day report cards came out. "You've always been an A student. Where did these B's and C's come from all of a sudden?"

"Maybe the schools here in Elmwood are more advanced than the ones out west," Aunt Alice suggested. "Perhaps they grade harder."

"In that case, Bruce should be working harder."

Mr. Walker had no patience with average-type marks. He knew that both Bruce and Liz were bright children and he had always expected them to stay at the top of their classes.

"I know I should, Dad." Bruce struggled to stifle a yawn. "I'll get at that math tonight."

"You look as though you could fall asleep right here at the table," his mother said worriedly. "Can't you do some of your studying in the afternoon, dear?" She turned to her husband. "He and Liz both go out to play right after school every day. They're out all afternoon, *every* afternoon."

"I'm not tired. It's only eight o'clock." Bruce forced his eyes wide. The last thing he wanted was to be forbidden to spend his afternoons outside the house. "I'm just sort of drowsy from eating so much. I'll wake right up as soon as I get going on that math."

But the math problems, when he opened his book to them, seemed to be written in a foreign language. There was no sense to any of them, even the simple ones. Numbers danced before Bruce's eyes like black dots, shifting and whirling about against the white page. By the time twenty minutes had passed he was fast asleep, his face buried in the book.

There was good reason for Bruce's weariness. Not only was he doing more outdoor physical work than he had ever done in his life, but he was getting up at five o'clock every morning. It was at this time of day that Red Rover had his exercise.

Exercising the small dogs was no problem. They could romp in the yard behind the hotel where the bushes were a protective screen cutting them off from the street. Every afternoon Liz took them outdoors for a play time, and they went out again after dinner.

Red Rover, however, was a different problem. He could not be satisfied with chasing a ball around a tiny, restricted area. Red was a big dog, a dog bred for running. As his wounds began to heal and his health and good spirits returned, so too did his energy. He roamed restlessly around the hotel, scratching at the doors and propping his big paws on the sills to gaze wistfully out windows. Sometimes he barked.

"That's not good," Tim said worriedly. "Even with the house set back like it is, sounds carry. Somebody might be walking past sometime and hear him."

"We can run him at night." It was Bruce who had come up with the idea. "That way there wouldn't be any chance of Jerry and his folks seeing him. I sleep on the fold-down sofa in the den. Everybody else in the family sleeps upstairs. I could slip out in the night after they're all asleep and nobody would know the difference."

"I wish I could help you," Tim said. "I feel like a heel not offering to do my half of it, but my bedroom is next to the girls'. There's always one of them hopping up and down for water or something. They'd catch me first thing and go tattling off to our folks."

"That's okay," Bruce said. "I don't mind doing it myself. I'll just set my alarm for two hours earlier than I usually get up and have Red out and back again before it gets light."

The first time he had tried this the alarm clock had gone off like a fire bell. The shrill sound had been so shattering through the silence of the sleeping house that both his parents and Aunt Alice had waked in terror.

"What was that? Did you hear that? Was it the doorbell?"

"A telephone?"

"Could someone have set off a burglar alarm?"

"I'm sure it was an air-raid siren!" screamed Aunt Alice. "I remember what they were like during the First World War! Oh dear, oh, dear, do you suppose someone has decided to attack us in the night?"

Lying huddled in his bed with the now-silent clock clutched protectively to his chest, Bruce heard their frantic voices as they rushed through the upstairs hall, pulling on robes, answering the phone, and finally running down the stairs to see if someone was at the front door.

After that, he kept the alarm clock under his pillow. This muffled the sound, and soon he grew so used to having it there that he began to waken at the first tiny click before the bell even had a chance to ring.

Getting out of bed was the hard part. Once he was into his clothes and out of the house, there was something very nice about being up and about before the rest of the world. The sky, still dotted with stars, and the cold, fresh smell of the air filled him with a special kind of excitement.

Raising the ramp against the window ledge, he would hear Red Rover stirring around inside, already awake and eager for his outing.

"Red?"

He never had to speak more than once. The big dog would be upon him, tail thumping excitedly, body quivering with anticipation.

Once they were outside, the world opened before them, theirs alone. It was night when they started off along the deserted streets, but soon the dark shapes of trees began to emerge against the gradually paling sky. Red was like a wild thing in the joy of his freedom, first racing ahead, then loping back to circle Bruce and fly off again in another direction.

Then, in what seemed a matter of minutes, it was

morning. The sky lightened in the east, turning from gray to a soft pink. Birds began to twitter in the trees, making drowsy, coming-awake noises. Somewhere a baby cried, the sound coming surprisingly loud through the stillness.

Then the sun itself appeared, a bright red ball over the treetops, and the whole sky exploded with color. It was so much brighter, so much more thrilling, Bruce thought in wonder, than it ever was in an evening sunset! This was the point at which he turned Red toward home.

As he told Tim, he did not mind these morning outings. It was fun being out alone with Red. It made him feel in a way as though he were his real master.

No matter how much he enjoyed himself, however, the fact remained that each morning he was giving up two hours of sleep. The rest of the day seemed to go on forever. Sitting in class, Bruce would find his head nodding, his eyes drooping. The sound of the teacher's voice would begin to drone like a lullaby, and before class was half over he would be fighting to keep himself awake.

Despite his exhaustion, Bruce did make an effort to do more studying. The grades on his first quarter report card had shocked him as much as they had his father. He was used to being at the top of his class, and to find himself making C's where he once had made A's was an upsetting experience.

Every night after dinner he spread his books out on the table in the den and tried to concentrate. Often he ended by falling asleep on top of them.

It was one of these times that his mother came in and found him there. She stood gazing down at him worriedly.

"I can't understand it," she said softly. "It's not even eight-thirty yet. Can he be sick, I wonder? Maybe I should make a doctor's appointment and see that he gets a complete check-up." Leaning over, she touched his arm. "Bruce, dear? You'd better go to bed. You're not going to get any studying done tonight."

Bruce mumbled something and turned his face against his outstretched arm.

"Come, dear, I'll help you."

Mrs. Walker put her arm around him and half lifted, half dragged him to his feet. Steering him to the bed, she helped him into it. Bruce was so heavily asleep the moment his head touched the pillow that he was not even aware of his mother's removing his shoes. She drew a blanket over him and quietly turned out the light.

The next day he woke to the pale light of early morning. For a long moment he lay there wondering what had happened. It had been weeks since he had wakened to anything but total darkness. Sliding his hand under the pillow, he groped for the clock. It was not there. Lifting his head, he saw it on the table next to the bed. Both hands pointed to the top — twelve o'clock midnight.

"How — why —"

And then the realization hit him. The clock had run down! It had been neither wound nor set. He had fallen asleep the night before without setting the alarm, and now it was morning.

"Good gosh! Poor Red!" Bruce sat up in bed, shocked wide awake. "He's probably over there tearing the walls down!"

Grabbing for the shoes which his mother had placed beside the bed, he began hurriedly to put them on. It was still early. It had to be. The light was still dim. He could hardly make out the blur of his jacket thrown across the back of the chair by the door. People in Elmwood were not generally early risers. Streets were free of cars until close to seven.

I can still give him a quick run, Bruce thought as he pulled on the jacket. The Bateses aren't going to be sitting on their lawn to watch the sun rise. We'll just take a fast trek down the street and back again. It won't be much for Red, but it will be better than nothing.

Heavy fog engulfed him as he left the house. He could hardly see ten feet before him, but by the time he reached the empty lot between the houses he could hear the short, sharp sounds of impatient barking.

When he reached the hotel, Red Rover was so happy to see him that he nearly knocked him over.

"Simmer down, boy. Calm down, old fellow." Bruce gave the leaping animal a quick pat. "This is going to be a short one this morning."

When he opened the door at the end of the hall the dog shot past him with the speed of a bullet. Up he went to the back window and down the ramp. By the time Bruce had followed him outside, he was nowhere to be seen.

"Red! Hey, Red, where are you?" Bruce called softly, keeping his voice low. "Red Rover, come on back here!"

Rounding the corner of the house, he crossed the front yard to the sidewalk. He looked up and down the street in both directions. Somewhere ahead of him a streak of red flashed across a yard and disappeared into the mists. Bruce began to run. He reached the yard and stopped.

"Red! Red Rover!" He called more loudly this time.

The fog was heavy, shutting off his view of the end of the street. A milk truck rattled by. The door of the house across the street from him opened, and a woman stuck out a head full of curlers.

"Here, kitty, kitty, kitty! Come get your breakfast!" Her voice was thin and shrill.

"It's later than I thought!" Bruce realized. "It's the fog. I didn't know —" A feeling of panic came over him. "I've got to get hold of Red! I've got to get him home fast!"

It was impossible to know with any certainty where the dog had gone. Bruce hurried along the sidewalk, glancing frantically into yards on either side. Every few paces he stopped to call Red's name.

"You looking for somebody?" a voice called to him. A newspaper boy pulled his bicycle to a stop next to the curb.

"Yes. No. I mean, it's not a person." Bruce did not know what to answer. "I'm looking for a —"

The newsboy was not listening. His attention was directed toward a side street.

"Look at that, will you!" he exclaimed. "It looks like one of those ghost hounds on TV."

Following his gaze, Bruce saw the outline of a dog against a bank of fog.

"It's not a ghost," he said. "It's —"

"Like a science fiction movie." The newsboy leaned forward. "Here he comes!"

Red Rover galloped toward them.

"That's no spirit dog!" the boy cried. "He sure looked like one for a minute. Hey, isn't that the setter that's been missing from that house down the street? The one they've put up a reward for?"

"I don't think so," Bruce said quickly, as Red shot past them. He was headed for home now. He had had his run and knew that breakfast awaited him back at the hotel.

"I bet it is," the boy said. "I sure wish I'd thought in time to grab him."

"It's not the same dog," Bruce said again. "I'm sure it's not. That dog used to live next door to me — the one that's lost, I mean. I've seen it. This dog here didn't look the same at all."

"Well, I think he did," the newsboy said. "I deliver papers to that house, so I've seen the setter. There can't be many big dogs like that running loose around the neighborhood."

He turned to Bruce, his eyes narrowing suspiciously. "Say, I bet I know what you've got in mind. You're trying to turn me off so you can go claim that reward yourself. Well, it's not going to work, kid!" He grinned triumphantly. "I'm going down to that house right now and tell them I've seen their ghost dog and the reward is *mine!*"

Chapter Ten

THE DAY THE PUPPIES ate a whole can of dog food and whined for more, Bruce pronounced them old enough to leave their mother.

"You'd better line up some homes for them fast," he told Liz, "before they eat up the whole hotel."

Although she had known all along that such a day would eventually arrive, Liz was heartbroken.

"Poor little things," she mourned to Debbie, as they walked to school together. "I should never have taught them to eat out of a dish. If they couldn't do that, Bruce couldn't make us get rid of them."

"I wish I could take one," Debbie said wistfully. She was spending much of her spare time at the hotel and had become very fond of the puppies. "That little Harry is such a darling. I'd much rather have him than Mom's darned old cat."

"It's not fair," Liz said. "If we have to send somebody away, why couldn't it be Red Rover? He eats ten times as much as those tiny puppies. But, no, Red is special, because Bruce and Tim are boys and they like big dogs better than little ones."

Despite her feelings she kept her promise and posted a notice about the puppies on the school bulletin board. She wrote it in the tiniest writing possible in hopes that no one would notice it crammed in among all the other items. She soon realized that this had been a bad mistake. The fact that the writing was so small that it could not be read easily made everyone who saw it curious as to what it said.

A small group gathered around the board, and other people as they passed pushed their way in to see what was so interesting. Before long the hallway in front of the bulletin board was jammed with students struggling to make out the message:

FREE PUPPIES. BROWN AND WHITE.

CAN BE DELIVERED TO YOUR HOME.

SEE LIZ WALKER, ROOM 207.

"Free puppies!" One girl let out a little squeal. "What fun! I wonder if Mother would let me have one!"

"It's my brother's birthday next Monday," another girl said. "He'll be eight years old. I bet he'd love to have a puppy."

"My dog was hit by a car a couple of months ago," a boy said sadly. "When that happened I felt like I'd never want another pet, but now — I don't know

— when you're used to having a dog around it gets kind of lonely without one."

When the bell rang for recess, Liz found four people waiting for her in the hall outside the classroom. The girl with the little brother and the boy whose dog had been run over were both definite about wanting puppies. Liz agreed to deliver them the next day. The other girl wanted to know how big they were, and when Liz told her she said that she liked small dogs and was almost sure she would take one but would have to check first to get her mother's permission.

The fourth person was from Liz's class, although she did not really know her. She was a thin, quiet, dark-haired girl named Annabel Higgins. Liz had always thought of Annabel as a little brown mouse. Now the mouse spoke.

"I saw your ad on the board," Annabel said in a wispy little voice.

"I guess everybody did," Liz said. As usual, when speaking to someone she did not know well, she heard her voice sounding cold and snippy, even though she did not mean for it to be that way. "I'm sorry, but you're too late to get one. They have already been promised."

"All of them!" Annabel exclaimed. "You're lucky! Our dog, Ginger, had five puppies a couple of months ago and we haven't been able to find homes for any of them. Ginger's a purebred Airedale, but

105

her husband was a bulldog. That's kind of a funny combination."

"All puppies are cute, no matter who their parents are," Liz said. "You're lucky if you *can't* find homes for them. I wish I could keep Sadie's puppies and watch them grow up."

"Oh, there's no chance of keeping them," Annabel said. "My father says one dog in the family is plenty. If we don't find homes for the pups soon he's going to drown them."

"He's going to *what?*" Liz was so horrified that she forgot to be stiff and awkward. She could not believe her ears. "Your father must be a horrid, unfeeling monster!"

"He's very strict," Annabel said, looking more like a mouse than ever. "He was hoping Ginger would have Airedale puppies so we could sell them for a lot of money. When she fell in love with the bulldog next door, Daddy just got furious. He says he doesn't want a lot of half-breed mutts around the place."

"He sounds like exactly the kind of man Jerry Bates will be when he grows up," Liz said hotly. "My dad's strict too, but he'd die before he'd hurt a helpless little puppy. You aren't going to let him, are you, Annabel? Can't you *do* something?"

"I don't know what," Annabel said forlornly. "When Daddy makes up his mind, that's it. Do you know anyone who would take a puppy?"

"I've used up all the people I know," Liz said. "What about putting an ad on the bulletin board the way I did? I bet you could get homes for all the pups right away."

"Do you really think so?" Annabel brightened. "That would be wonderful. What should I say?"

"Don't say they're part bulldog," Liz said firmly. "Let people figure that out for themselves. If you have to say anything, you can say they're a large part Airedale."

Annabel looked doubtful. "They're not, though. They're just *half* Airedale."

"Oh, for goodness sake," Liz said disgustedly, "that's a large enough part," and catching Annabel's hand, she dragged her down the hall to the bulletin board.

There was no group standing in front of the board this time. There was just one person, Mr. Caton, the school principal. He had taken down Liz's notice and was holding it in his hand, reading it.

He raised his eyes as the girls came up to him. "Good morning, girls," he said. "Does either of you happen to know who this Liz Walker is?"

Liz hesitated a moment. If Annabel had not been with her she might have been tempted to say no. As it was, however, this was hardly possible.

"I am, sir," she said in a small voice.

"Then you're the one who put this on the board this morning?" Mr. Caton was frowning. His brows drew together across the top of his nose in a straight gray line. "Don't you know that this is a board for school notices? It's to be used only for class meetings and sports events and activity lists and so forth."

"I'm sorry," Liz said. "I didn't know. I mean, I didn't really think —"

"No notices of any kind can be posted on this board without my permission," the principal said.

"I'm sorry, sir," Liz said again.

She glanced at Annabel, who was twisting her hands together nervously. It was obvious that she was not going to say anything.

"Please, sir," she said quickly, before she could lose her nerve, "could we have permission to post another notice? I don't need this one up any longer because all our puppies have been spoken for, but my friend here has five of them and if we don't find homes for them right away her father is going to drown them."

"That's a sad situation." Mr. Caton's expression softened. For a moment Liz thought he was going to say, "All right."

Then slowly he shook his head. "Even in this case," he said regretfully, "I can't let you use the school bulletin board for a personal notice. If I let you do it, I'd have to, in fairness, let everybody else too. Everyone has something he would like to advertise. Pretty soon we'd need ten boards to hold all the ads for dogs and cats and rabbits and goldfish."

His words were reasonable. There was no way to argue with them. Even if there had been, fifth graders don't get anywhere arguing with a school principal. Still, to Liz, *nothing* was reasonable if it meant the lives of five puppies.

She worried about them all afternoon. As she turned the pages of her history book she saw, instead of pictures of United States presidents, five sad little Airedale-bulldog faces. When she glanced across at Annabel, bent over her own book, she felt like grabbing something and throwing it at her. How could she just sit there like that and do nothing?

If they were my puppies, I'd certainly think of some way to save them, Liz thought bitterly. If I couldn't find homes for them, I'd hide them and raise them secretly. I'd train them to do tricks, and when they were grown I'd sell them to a circus.

The more she thought about it, the better that idea seemed to her. Surely the funnier-looking a dog was, the better a circus would like it. The whole idea of a circus was to make people laugh. Training dogs was not too difficult either. She had trained Bebe to chase a ball and to roll over. It could not be much harder to teach more circusy things, such as walking a high wire and dancing and jumping through hoops.

By the time the final bell rang, Liz was bursting with excitement.

"Annabel!" she cried, rushing to catch up with her. "Wait a minute! I have a wonderful idea!"

Annabel turned hopefully, but after Liz had explained the plan to her, she did not look enthusiastic.

"I don't know," she said. "I've never trained a dog. Besides, I don't know where I'd hide them."

"Don't worry about those things." Liz brushed the problems aside. "I have a place where we can keep them, and I'll help with the training. All you have to do is keep it a secret until they're ready to give a performance."

Debbie, when Liz told her about it, did not echo her friend's confidence,

"Annabel's an awful baby about things," she said. "It's hard to imagine her keeping a secret if somebody tried to make her tell it."

"I know," Liz said. "I don't like that part of it either. Still we have to save those puppies. I haven't even seen them, and I love them already just the way I do Tom and Dick and Harry."

"I guess you're right," Debbie agreed with a sigh. "We'll just have to take the chance."

When they reached Annabel's house that afternoon and saw the puppies, they had no doubts that what they were doing was right. The pups were big ones, much larger than Sadie's, with shaggy Airedale hair and square bulldog faces, but their stubby tails never stopped wagging. They tumbled and rolled

and bounced, falling over their feet to be the first
to greet their guests.

"What clowns!" Liz picked up the nearest puppy
and hugged it while the rest swarmed about her, yip-
ping in jealousy. "We'll give them the big, green
bedroom upstairs right next to MacTavish."

"When your father comes home tonight," Debbie
said to Annabel, "you tell him you gave the puppies
to friends of yours, but don't you dare say who the
friends were or what they're going to do with them."

Getting the puppies to the hotel was not easy.
There were so many of them, and they were so
wiggly and squirmy. There was an alley behind
Annabel's house that ran the length of the block,
but beyond that there was only the sidewalk. Liz
and Debbie each carried two puppies and Annabel one. Everybody they passed turned to stare at
them.

"Where are you going?" one lady asked. "To a
dog show?"

A mother with a baby came by, and the baby
squealed, "Kitty! Kitty!" and nearly fell out of his
stroller.

"Those aren't kitties, dear," the mother explained
to him, "they're doggies. And such a lot of them."

But the baby kept shrieking, "Kitty! Kitty!" all
the way down the street until his mother took him
around a corner.

Two little boys passed on bicycles, waving and

shouting. The puppies yipped back at them and squirmed delightedly. They would have loved to be able to get down and chase the bikes.

"Well, we're almost there," Debbie panted, as they came to the final block. "Just a little further and — oh, no!"

"What is it?" Liz asked, and turned her head to see where Debbie was looking.

Now it was her turn to say, "Oh, no!" Coming toward them along the sidewalk was Jerry Bates.

Chapter Eleven

HE WAS BY HIMSELF. That was the first thing that
Liz noticed. He did not look nearly as important
somehow when he was alone as he did when he was
surrounded by his gang of followers.

Come to think of it, I haven't seen any kids going
in or out of his house for quite a while now, she
thought suddenly. She did not have time to take the
thought further because Jerry had reached them.

"Well, what do we have here?" He stopped in
front of them, blocking the sidewalk. Surprisingly
he seemed almost glad to see them. "What are you
doing with those dogs, Liz? Your aunt's allergic to
them. She told my father so when he got me Red
Rover."

"They're not my dogs," Liz said steadily, her arms
tightening protectively around the puppies. "They
belong to Annabel. We're hunting for homes for them.
We're going to knock on doors up and down the street
to see if anybody wants them."

The moment she had said it, she realized that it was not a bad idea at all. Why *not* knock on doors and see if anyone wanted a puppy? The fewer there were when they reached the hotel with them, the less dog food it would take to raise them.

"They're pretty funny looking," Jerry said. He reached out a finger and poked at one of the puppies. "Nobody with any sense is going to want a mutt like this."

"They're not mutts at all," Liz said furiously. "These are purebred Bulldales! They're the latest breed! All the movie stars have them! They're winning all the prizes in dog shows these days!"

"They are?" Jerry looked skeptical, but there was a flicker of interest in his eyes. "If they're that great, how come you haven't been able to give any of them away?"

"We have," Liz said, glad that Bruce was not there to hear her. "We've given away five of them already just since school was out. See, there are only five left where there used to be ten!"

"They're really going that fast?" Jerry tried not to show it, but his interest was increasing. He studied the pups for a long moment. Suddenly he smiled. It was the bright, sweet smile he usually used with grown-ups.

"Well, I guess I'll help you out. I'll take that one," and he pointed to the largest puppy, which was one of the two Debbie was carrying.

For a moment there was silence. Everyone was too astonished to speak.

Then Liz said explosively, "You certainly will not!"

"Liz!" Annabel turned to her in bewilderment. "What are you saying? Isn't that what we want most — to find the puppies homes?"

"Not with somebody like Jerry Bates," Liz said firmly. "I wouldn't send a mountain lion to live at the Bateses' house."

"Look here!" Jerry's handsome face flushed with anger. "You just finished telling me these aren't your puppies! They belong to this girl here. I want a dog, and she wants me to have one, and I don't see why you should have anything to say about it."

"Annabel does not want you to have one!" Debbie exclaimed. She turned to Annabel. "Don't you dare give him a puppy! Jerry tortured his last dog until it ran away. Bruce and Tim have told me all about it."

"He didn't run away," Jerry said. "Somebody stole him. That somebody lives right in this neighborhood too! Our newsboy saw Red the other morning. He said he looked like a ghost running through the fog, but he recognized him and was sure it was Red Rover."

"You beat that poor dog and tied a rope around his neck that almost strangled him!" Liz cried. "It's a wonder he didn't break his back trying to run with that wagon behind him. In fact —" She forced herself to stop before she said too much.

Jerry was watching her intently. "In fact what?" he asked. "You seem to know a lot about my dog. What 'fact' were you going to tell me?"

"In fact —" Liz realized that she had gone too far. Frantically she searched her mind for some way to end her sentence. "In fact," she brought out slowly, "I bet you *did* break his back. I bet he ran off someplace and dug a hole for himself and got in it and died. I bet it *was* a ghost that newsboy saw."

"That's crazy." Clearly Jerry had not been expecting anything like this. "Dogs can't be ghosts. They don't have souls."

"How do you know they don't?" Liz shot back at him. "A dog like Red Rover has more of a soul than you'll ever have. I bet he's a ghost, and I hope he comes through your walls at night and haunts you!"

With that she clutched the two puppies she was holding tightly against her chest and marched right past Jerry and on down the street.

At the corner the other two girls caught up with her. Debbie grabbed her arm and squeezed it triumphantly.

"Oh, Liz, you were great! How do you ever think up such things! You should have seen his face after you walked off like that! He turned pale!"

"How could you lie like that?" Annabel asked in a shocked voice. "You made all that up, Liz Walker, about there being ten puppies and all the movie stars having them — it wasn't any of it true at all!"

"I know," Liz admitted. "Now, come on, let's cut through our side yard and go to the hotel from the back so that Jerry won't see us."

When the girls reached the hotel, Bruce and Tim were there already. Tim saw them first. He was coming down the stairs carrying MacTavish's water bowl.

"Where have you been so long?" he asked irritably. "School's been out for an hour! Bruce and I have had to do all your housework, changing the sandboxes and filling the water bowls and —"

He broke off suddenly when he saw what Liz was carrying.

"Oh, my gosh! Bruce, come see what your crazy sister has brought with her!"

"It better not be another dog!" Bruce came in from the den with Red Rover at his heels. "One more bottomless pit like MacTavish to feed and we'll be broke!" His eyes widened in disbelief. "Oh, my gosh, *five of them!* And who's *that?*"

"She's Annabel Higgins," Liz said. "Annabel, this is my brother Bruce and that's Tim Kelly."

"You know we agreed not to bring in any more partners!" Bruce said. "And five new dogs —"

"But I've found homes for Sadie's puppies," Liz said quickly. "So really, it's just two more dogs than before, not five, and we have grand plans for these. We're going to train them for the circus."

"They look like circus dogs, that's for sure." Tim took Annabel's puppy from her and set it on the floor. "Here, Red, come meet a new friend!"

Red Rover began to wag his tail as he sniffed at the puppy. Bruce's attention was still on his sister.

"What if somebody had seen you bringing those dogs in here, Liz? What if that person told Aunt Alice or Dad or Mother? How long do you think we could keep our hotel going if they found out about it? About two minutes, that's how long!"

"Jerry Bates did see us," Debbie said. "You should have heard Liz take care of him! She scared him green, Bruce."

Delightedly she recited the story of Liz's conversation with Jerry. When she had finished Tim was grinning broadly and even Bruce was beginning to smile a little.

"You couldn't really have scared him," Bruce said. "It was a good try, but nobody would believe that ghost-dog story. I'm sure he didn't really turn pale."

"I don't know about that," Tim said. His blue eyes were sparkling with laughter. "Jerry *does* believe in ghosts. I found out one time when some of us guys were kidding around telling ghost stories. Jerry didn't want any part of it. He really acted nervous."

"Well, maybe you did scare him then," Bruce said to his sister. "I wish I could have been there to hear it. Still, that doesn't solve the problem of all this extra mob to feed. We don't have the money, and you know it, and you had no business bringing them home."

"We could advertise in the newspaper," Debbie suggested.

Bruce shook his head. "That costs money, too. Besides, you have to give an address so people can pick up the dogs. Whose address could we give? Not this one. Not Aunt Alice's."

"It's the middle of November already," Liz said. "We get our allowances December first. We can use those for dog food. I won't spend even a penny on anything else this time."

"What about Christmas?" Bruce asked her. Aren't you going to buy any presents for anyone?"

"I'll write everybody poems for presents," Liz said recklessly. Then she paused. She had forgotten that she was finished with writing poetry. "I'll sew things. Pin cushions and pen wipers."

"You'll have to buy material," Bruce reminded her. He sighed. "Face it, kids, it just won't work. We're getting in deeper and deeper. The leaves are finished falling now, and there isn't any snow to shovel yet, and Tim and I are about through earning money. What are we going to do?"

A soft voice spoke. "What about charging room rent?"

Everyone turned to stare at Annabel. They had almost forgotten she was there.

"Room rent!" Bruce said. "How can the dogs pay rent? The whole reason they're here is that they don't have owners."

"But lots of dogs do," Annabel said. Her voice seemed to gather assurance as the idea took hold of her. "People go out of town and don't have anywhere to leave their pets. I know when we went away last summer we had to leave Ginger in a kennel. They charged two dollars a day."

"Two dollars a day!" Tim let out a low whistle. "My gosh, that's fourteen dollars a week. If we charged half that, it would still be a lot of money!"

"Think how many cans of dog food." Liz's eyes were shining. "Oh, Annabel, that's a fabulous idea!"

"And I know just who to get for the first guest," Debbie cried excitedly. "Mary Ann Martin's dog, Preston. The Martins are flying to visit their grandmother for Thanksgiving vacation. They'll have to leave Preston someplace — why not with us?"

"You'll have to make it sound as though it's just with *you*," Liz said. "They can't know it's a hotel."

"Of course not. But I know the Martins. I've been to Mary Ann's lots of times. I know they'd rather leave Preston with me than at a kennel where he'll have to stay in a cage and won't have anybody to play with him," Debbie said confidently.

Annabel was standing quietly with her hands clasped in front of her, but there was a proud smile on her face.

Bruce smiled at her and then at his sister. For the first time in weeks the worry lines were smoothed out of his forehead and he looked like the brother Liz had always known.

"You know," he said, "this just might work. Our new partner, Annabel, might have had the idea that will keep us from going out of business!"

Chapter Twelve

MARY ANN MARTIN's dog, Preston, was a beagle.

"Just think," Liz said, "he'll be the first beagle to stay at our hotel!"

Debbie brought Preston over on Wednesday, the day before Thanksgiving. School was out at noon as a prelude to the Thanksgiving holidays, and the hotel staff were all waiting to greet him.

Preston was a lively dog and terribly strong for his size. He raced up the ramp so fast that Debbie, who was holding his leash, nearly fell on her face.

"He's a hunting beagle," she explained, handing the leash to Bruce with relief. "I guess there are two kinds, the hunters and the stay-at-homes. Mary Ann's father is training Preston to hunt rabbits. That must be why his legs are so strong."

Preston was so excited at the sight and smell of so many other dogs that he tore around in circles. He ran from one hotel room to another giving little yelps and bounded up the stairs and came tearing down again like a wild thing.

"He sure is a lively one," Tim commented. He looked a little worried. "I hope he doesn't upset the others."

"The other dogs are used to each other," Liz said. "Sadie and Red have been friends for a long time now, and MacTavish is so fat and easygoing he likes everybody. The pups are too young to get upset about anything except not eating on time."

"Still," Tim said, frowning, "I don't much like the idea of leaving Preston free to roam around the hotel. Let's put him in his room until he calms down a little."

They had decided to give Preston MacTavish's room on the second floor and to move the terrier in with Sadie, who was lonely now that Tom, Dick, and Harry had gone. Tim had objected at first (he always tended to favor MacTavish), but since Preston was a paying guest Liz had insisted that it was only right that he have his own accommodations.

It took some time to get Preston settled into his room as the smell of MacTavish was still very much in it. Preston had evidently never had much experience with other dogs, and he rushed about sniffing everything excitedly.

"Perhaps he's looking for rabbits," Annabel suggested.

It was past one o'clock by the time Preston finally

settled down on his bed for a nap and Bruce felt that they could go off and leave him. As they walked toward home they noticed that the drapes behind the windows of the yellow house next to Aunt Alice's were open and there was a car parked in the driveway.

"I guess that means we won't be able to cut through their yard anymore," Liz said regretfully. "I wonder where they've been for so long."

"Aunt Alice was saying something to Mother about their being retired people who travel a lot." Bruce looked worried. "I wish they'd kept on traveling a while longer. They might start wondering what we're going back and forth all the time for, and if the dogs should start barking —"

"They don't bark much," Liz said. "They're really very well behaved." The hotel was earning money, and the problem of supporting the dogs was solved at last. She did not intend to ruin things by starting right in worrying about something new.

Lunch was on the table waiting when they got home to Aunt Alice's.

"I expected you before this," their mother said. "I had the idea school was out at noon today."

Aunt Alice's nose began to twitch as she fought off a sneeze.

"Goodness," she said, "if I didn't know better I would say there was dog hair in this room. I think I'm going to — going to — going to — Atchooooo!"

"Bless you," Liz said, and hurriedly brushed at the hairs on her sweater. The other dogs at the hotel were kept carefully brushed, but Preston had been shedding.

They had just sat down to their soup and sandwiches when the telephone rang. Mrs. Walker answered. When she came back to the table she was smiling.

"That was Dad calling from work," she said. "Guess what? His training program will be over the beginning of December, and he's been assigned to his new office."

"You mean you'll be moving that soon?" Aunt Alice's round face grew sober. "I've been looking forward so much to having you here for Christmas. Life gets lonely for an old lady when the holidays come around. There have been many times lately when I've wished that Peter and I had had children. Of course, at the time we were so involved in our work —"

Bruce and Liz, who had had their mouths open to cheer, let them drop closed in astonishment. For months now all they had thought about was how grand it would be to move out of this crowded house where all the ways of doing things were so different from their own. It had never occurred to them that their being here might mean something special to Aunt Alice.

And her work — had Aunt Alice actually had a job when she was younger? It was hard to imagine this fluttery, white-haired little woman ever being anything other than a housewife. Had she been a secretary, perhaps, or a bookkeeper or a saleslady for a dress store? Impossible!

Mrs. Walker's face grew gentle. "Why, Aunt Alice," she said, "I'm glad you feel that way. We wouldn't want to have Christmas without you either, and we won't have to. We won't be moving very far. The new office is going to be right here in Elmwood!"

It was then that they heard the sound. It started low and rose slowly, note by note, into a long, wretched wail.

The smile faded from Mrs. Walker's face. "My goodness, what's that? It sounds like a siren."

"A siren!" Aunt Alice's plump face grew pale. "Another air-raid warning just like the one we heard last month. Oh, dear, oh, dear, this time it must really mean war!"

"It's not the same though," Mrs. Walker said. She was listening intently. "That sound we heard in the night was like an alarm going off. This is more of a — a sort of — howl. It sounds almost like a hound on the trail of a rabbit."

Bruce and Liz exchanged helpless glances as the deep, mournful voice of the beagle rose again, longer and louder this time.

"It is a hound!" their mother exclaimed. "I'd know that sound anyplace. My father used to have one when

I was a little girl. That's the way they howl when they're hunting or when they're cooped up somewhere and want to get out."

"But nobody in this neighborhood owns a hound," Aunt Alice said. "At least, I've never heard of one. Do you children know of anyone with a hunting dog?"

"No," Liz said weakly.

Bruce thought desperately. "Maybe it's in a car parked someplace," he said. "I could go look."

He was out of his seat and halfway across the room before his mother could stop him.

"Don't be silly, dear. Come back to the table and finish your lunch. If someone has left a dog in a car, it's none of our business. If that noise keeps up long enough to really bother people, I imagine the police will investigate."

"The police!" Bruce exclaimed in horror.

"Disturbing the peace," Aunt Alice said. "They have big fines for that."

"I'm through eating." Liz laid her napkin on the table beside her plate. Without ever having met the elderly couple in the yellow house, she could picture them clearly, standing by their telephone, looking up the number of the police station. If Preston's howls were this loud here, what must they be like one house closer!

"Please," she said, "may I be excused?"

The beagle's voice rose, wavered, fell, and rose, wavered and fell again. Then, suddenly, the sound stopped.

"Well," Mrs. Walker said, "someone must have investigated and let the poor thing out."

"Please," Liz repeated frantically, "may I be excused? Please, Mother, Aunt Alice — I'm really *finished*."

"I am too," Bruce said. "Honestly, I couldn't eat another bite."

"Oh, all right," their mother said with a little laugh. "I guess all the excitement of Thanksgiving vacation does make things kind of special. Run along and play, and make up for it by eating a big . . ."

They did not stay to hear the end of the sentence. The first three words were hardly out of her mouth when both children were out of the house and running wildly down the street toward the hotel.

They had almost reached the ramp when they saw the figure of the boy standing near it. He had his head cocked on one side, listening intently. Bruce stopped short, and Liz, who was right behind him, nearly ran into him.

"Oh, no," she breathed. "Not him again! Not here — not now!"

Jerry Bates turned to face them. "What are you doing here?" he asked.

"We — we're —" Bruce began haltingly. Then he

stopped himself. Why should he make excuses to Jerry? This was not his property either. "We've got as much right here as you do," he said.

"I heard a dog howling," Jerry said. "It sounded like Red. Somebody in this neighborhood's stolen my dog, and I'm going to find out who it is."

"Well, you certainly can't think we took him," Liz said. "Where could we keep him? You know Aunt Alice is allergic to animals."

"I do know that," Jerry said. "If it weren't for that, I *would* think it was you. Things have been going funny ever since you two moved into this neighborhood."

"How do you mean, 'funny'?" Bruce asked uncomfortably.

From where he stood he could see the ramp leaning up to the window. It was half hidden by bushes, and the shadows of the trees fell across it, but it was still there, perfectly evident to anyone who knew where to look for it. Jerry's back was toward it now, but if he should turn around —

"All kinds of things are funny," Jerry said. "First Red disappears. Then Tim quits the gang. Then I see you guys walking across the street carrying lumber, the same boards Tim was going to contribute toward a clubhouse, and still, I can't see you've built anything with them. Then your nutty sister comes by with five purebred Bulldales, and where are they now? She said she was giving them away.

I can't see that anybody on the street has one. And then the rest of the gang quits —"

"The rest of the gang?" Bruce repeated in bewilderment.

"Don't pretend you don't know about it. After Tim quit the gang, the rest of the guys, one by one, started falling out too. What have you and Tim been bribing them with? You don't either of you have anything like the stuff I have."

"Bruce doesn't bribe people with anything," Liz said hotly. "He doesn't have to. People like Bruce just because he's *Bruce*. Did you ever think that maybe your gang just got sick of the way you treat people?"

"That dog howling —" Jerry began.

"You think it's Red Rover!" Now that she had started, Liz could no more have stopped talking than she could have turned off a waterfall. All the anger she had ever felt at Jerry Bates came pouring out. "Well, I think so too. It *is* Red Rover. It's his poor beaten-up ghost howling for revenge, that's what it is. If I were you I'd run home and hide in a closet, Jerry Bates, and lock all the doors and windows, because the very worst ghosts in the whole world are dogs."

Jerry's face grew white.

"That's a lie," he said shakily. "Dogs don't have ghosts. I wish you'd never come to Elmwood, you Walkers! Everything was great until you came on the scene. Why didn't you stay back where you belonged?"

"We belong in Elmwood," Bruce said. "We like it here."

To his amazement, he realized that what he was saying was true. He turned to Liz, and he could see by her face that it was true for her too.

"Bruce is right," she said. "We have friends here now. It's home. Even if you're not born in a place, it starts being home as soon as you have friends."

"You're going to need every friend you've got," Jerry said tightly. "I got rid of one kid in this neighborhood I didn't like. Well, I can get rid of two more of them just as easily. You wait and see!" Turning on his heel, he stalked away.

Bruce and Liz stood silently until he had disappeared from view. Then, with one accord, they rushed for the ramp. A moment later they were inside the hotel, hurrying down the hall toward the stairway.

Tim was sitting on the steps with MacTavish on one side of him and Preston on the other.

"Hi," he said. "I see you finally got here."

"So you're the reason that darned beagle stopped howling." Bruce drew a long breath of relief. "We ran into Jerry out behind the hotel and got hung up talking to him. I was scared to death that dog would let out another blast right then."

"And the people in the yellow house are back,"

Liz added. "I was afraid *they* might have come over
here and found Preston."

"You mean the Smiths?" Tim grinned. "No
worry there. They're a real nice old couple but they're
both of them so hard of hearing they wouldn't know
it if Preston was howling right in their bedroom."
Then his face sobered. "Other people would know,
though. I could hear him all the way over at my
house. I guess beagles just don't like being left in
strange places. We can't risk this happening again.

One of us is going to have to stay here all the time until we get him back to his owner."

"At night too?" Liz exclaimed. "How can we?"

"Bruce and I can take turns," Tim said. "I'll tell my folks one night that I'm spending the night at his house, and the next time he can tell your folks that he's spending the night with me. During the daytime you girls can take turns dog-sitting."

"I don't like to lie to my parents," Bruce said worriedly. "Still, with Jerry snooping around like this —"

"I have an idea," Liz said softly.

Both boys turned to look at her.

"What kind of an idea?" Bruce asked warily.

"An idea that will keep him from bothering us forever. An idea that will keep him from ever hurting any helpless animal again." Liz's eyes were shining. "Oh, it's the best idea I've ever had in my life! Bruce, that picture you took of Red the first day we were in Elmwood — has that been developed yet?"

"Why, yes, I got the slides back last week," Bruce told her. "What does that have to do with anything?"

"It has everything to do with it," Liz said eagerly. "Tim said the Smiths wouldn't know it if a dog howled right in their bedroom. But Jerry would know it. There's nothing deaf about Jerry."

Her voice was squeaking with excitement.

"Tonight the ghost of Red Rover is going to get his revenge!"

Chapter Thirteen

THEY PLANNED IT for midnight.

"After all," Liz said, "midnight is the spookiest time. Besides, everyone will be asleep by then — Mother and Dad and Aunt Alice and all the Bateses."

"Are you sure you can get the projector?" Tim asked.

"That will be easy," Bruce told him. "Dad lets me use it whenever I want to. All I have to do is ask him to let me show some slides this evening after dinner and then not return it till tomorrow. What about an extension cord?"

"I can get that," Tim said. "We have a lot of them."

They grinned at each other excitedly, hardly able to believe the thing they were going to do. It was truly, as Liz had said, the best idea she had ever come up with.

"We'll have to get Debbie," she said now. "She

should be in on it, too. Why don't I invite her to spend the night? I know Mother will let me. Aunt Alice says she likes having children around."

"I'll tell my folks I'm spending the night with Bruce," Tim said, "and then I'll go over to the hotel and dog-sit Preston. At a quarter to twelve I'll meet you in front of your house." His blue eyes were sparkling. "Do you think it will really work?"

"Of course, it will work," Liz said decidedly. "It has to!"

That evening was the longest that Bruce and Liz had ever lived through. Even the fact that Debbie was with them, having been given permission to eat dinner there and spend the night, did not make the hours move any faster. After the dishes were cleared away, Bruce suggested showing slides, and Mr. Walker happily agreed. They spent an hour looking at pictures of Albuquerque — of the big adobe house where they had lived, of the mountains stretching purple tips into the sky, of the trees and arroyos of the West. The last slide in the batch that Bruce showed was of a little brown dachshund with a pointed face.

"That's Bebe," Liz said softly. Suddenly all the old homesickness for her pet flooded through her, as sharp and painful as it had been the day she had said good-bye. "Oh, I wish she were here now — I miss her so!"

"You'll be seeing her soon, dear," Mrs. Walker

said, smiling. "Now that we know we're in Elmwood to stay we'll find a place of our own and get settled and send for Bebe to be flown out on the very next plane."

"Are those all the slides you have, son?" Mr. Walker asked, as Bruce turned off the projector and reached for the light. "Haven't you taken any pictures since we got to Elmwood?"

"Well — yes," Bruce said, "but — well — I thought we could look at those another night. It's about bedtime now, isn't it?"

"Already?" His mother looked surprised. "Since Liz has a guest and tomorrow's a holiday, I thought you might want to stay up a little later than usual and pop some corn and play games the way we used to back in Albuquerque."

"That's all right, Mother," Liz said hastily. "Debbie and I are tired, too. I think we should all go to bed right now."

"That's a good idea," Debbie agreed, giving a great yawn. "I'm awfully sleepy. I'm used to going to bed very early."

"Well, all right," Mrs. Walker said, looking more surprised than ever. "I know Bruce has been tired lately, but you girls too? They must be working you terribly hard in school these days. I wonder if we should talk to the teachers. It just doesn't seem right — "

She was still worrying out loud to Mr. Walker

when the three children left the room to go to bed.

Any other night Bruce would have slept the moment his head touched the pillow. Tonight, though, things were different. He could hear the alarm clock ticking through the pillow right into his ear as it always did, but he was too keyed up to let it tick him into slumber. Instead he lay there listening, wide awake and alert to everything around him.

He could hear his parents and Aunt Alice talking in the living room. How long, he wondered, would they stay up? He could hear the trees rustling outside his window. He could even hear his own heart beating strongly against his chest.

It seemed forever before he heard the adults' footsteps on the stairs and their voices pitched low as they bid each other good-night.

How long would it take them to go to sleep? Lying in bed, he counted the seconds, making them into minutes, sixty seconds to one minute, sixty minutes to one hour. Flicking on the bedside light, he pulled the clock out from under his pillow and looked at the dial. Only a quarter to eleven. One whole hour to go.

He was sure that Liz and Debbie were lying awake in Liz's narrow bed in the sewing room, whispering together, too excited to sleep — just as he was. He wished they were here with him so they could at least share their waiting.

"It will never get there," he told himself, looking

at the minute hand stuck solidly in place against the face of the clock. "I'll lie here forever and it will never ever move." But as it turned out, some time between then and a quarter to twelve he fell asleep, and it took the muffled jangle of the alarm to bring him to.

He had been sleeping so hard that for a moment he thought it was five o'clock and time for Red's dawn run. Then, almost immediately, he remembered. Getting quickly out of bed, he pulled on the clothes which he had laid out on the chair beside him.

The light was on in the front hallway, and the girls were there already waiting for him.

"We never even took our clothes off," Liz told him. "We just pulled the blankets up over them. We've been counting the minutes on Debbie's watch."

Bruce shushed her with a finger against his lips. They put on their jackets in silence.

Debbie whispered, "The projector?"

It was standing by the front door where Bruce had left it. He drew a quick breath of relief that his father had not noticed it there and put it away himself.

Picking it up with one hand, he opened the door with the other, and the three children slipped outside into the night.

The moment the door was shut behind them, the darkness closed in from all sides.

Debbie gave a little gasp. "It's so black! We'll never find our way."

There was a sudden burst of light, and Tim spoke. "I brought a flashlight. Are you all set?" His voice was gruff with suppressed excitement.

"Did you bring the extension cord?" Bruce asked him.

"Sure did. A real long one. Where can we plug it?"

"The Bateses have an outdoor outlet on the side of the house," Bruce said. "I've seen Mr. Bates plug in his electric grill there. Shine the light ahead of us and follow me."

Moving quietly, they crossed the lawn and stepped into the Bateses' side yard. The outlet was exactly where Bruce had thought it was. Tim plugged in the extension cord and attached the projector to the receiving end.

"I hope it's long enough," Debbie whispered.

"So do I," Tim said. "I didn't realize the outlet was quite so far from Jerry's bedroom window. We'll just have to see."

With Bruce carrying the projector, they continued along the wall of the house. The ground-level window of Jerry's room loomed ahead of them. When they reached it they stopped.

"Are you sure this is his bedroom?" Liz asked doubtfully. "Does he really sleep in the basement?"

"If you could see the room, you'd forget it was

part of a basement," Tim told her. "It's like a private den with a bed in it."

Dropping to his knees, he pressed his face close to the window. "It's pitch black in there. He's sure to be sleeping. Are you ready with the projector?"

"Ready," Bruce said.

Crouching beside Tim, he sat the machine in place and felt in his pocket for the slide. For a moment he was afraid he had not brought it with him. Then his fingers closed around it, and with a breath of relief he inserted it in the projector.

"Okay," he said tensely. "We're ready. Let's hear it, Liz — the ghost of old Red! Loud enough to wake Jerry but not loud enough for his parents."

Liz drew a deep breath. Then she opened her mouth and let out a howl. She started low, just as Preston had that afternoon, and let the long, mournful wail rise in her throat, higher and higher. The result was so weird and chilling that Bruce felt shivers go up his spine even though he knew it was only his sister.

"Lean closer," he whispered. "The window is open about halfway. Let him have it full blast. He's got to be an awfully heavy sleeper to sleep through that!"

Crowding in between the two boys, Liz howled again, her mouth close to the opening in the window.

From inside the room came a muffled, sleepy voice, "What the devil — that crazy noise again — "

"He's awake!" Debbie whispered excitedly. "Now, Bruce! *Now!*"

Bruce pressed the button to operate the projector. The beam of light shot through the window over Jerry's bed and fell upon the wall directly across from him. At first it was just a blur of light and color. In the reflected glow, they could see Jerry directly beneath the window, sitting up in bed.

"What's happening?" he said, the sleep gone from his voice. "What's that? Who — where —"

"Howl!" Bruce whispered, and Liz howled. It was the best howl so far. It rose and rose in a frightful wail and ended with a wild tearing sound, like an animal in agonizing pain.

At the same instant, Bruce brought the projector into focus. The blur of light steadied and into the middle of it, sharp and clear, came the face of Red Rover.

Bruce had snapped the picture with the dog looking directly into the camera. The proud head was lifted into the sunlight, the mouth was open slightly, showing straight white teeth. To Jerry it must have seemed as though the huge brown eyes were staring accusingly into his very soul.

For a long moment there was no sound from the room in the basement. Then suddenly there was a great shriek. It was so loud and terrified that the four listeners, crouched on the ground outside the window, nearly jumped out of their skins.

"Mom!" Jerry yelled. "Dad! Help! Help! Come here quick!"

The windows of the front room on the second floor went bright with lights.

"Hurry, Bruce," Tim whispered frantically. "His folks are up!"

Bruce flicked off the light of the projector. "Run!" he whispered. "Run!"

No one had to be told twice. The girls were already at the boundary line that separated the Bateses'

house from Aunt Alice's. Tim was close behind them. Jerry's voice filled the darkness in frantic shouts for his parents.

Scrambling to his feet, Bruce started after the others. He had almost caught up with them when he felt the projector jerked from his hands. To his horror, he heard it go crashing to the ground.

"Oh, no!" With a gasp of dismay, he knelt down and began groping about in the darkness. His hands closed upon the machine. He lifted it, and it rattled in his hands. A dark shape appeared beside him. Tim had come back to help him.

"What happened?" he asked.

"I forgot to unplug it," Bruce told him. "It was crazy, but when Jerry started yelling I just ran and when I came to the end of the cord, the projector snapped out of my grip. I've smashed it."

"Well, there's no sense in worrying now," Tim said. "If it's broken it's broken. Come on, let's hurry! They'll be out here any minute to investigate."

The Bateses' house was now ablaze with lights, upstairs and down. Every room seemed to have lights in it. Jerry's voice could still be heard shouting something about, "Red's ghost! He's come back to get me!" Other voices, the soft mother tones, the lower father ones, floated across the lawn from the bedroom window.

Bruce got to his feet, clutching the projector tightly against him.

"It's Dad's projector," he said. "My gosh, Tim — and the cord —" He felt for the place where the electric cord fitted through the metal casing.

"Come on," Tim urged him. "We've got to run, Bruce! Do you hear me?"

He whirled and broke away into the darkness, with Bruce behind him. Just as they rounded the corner of Aunt Alice's house, the door of the Bateses' house opened.

Mr. Bates stepped out and flicked a switch which turned on the floodlights, illuminating the whole back yard.

"Now we'll see what this monkey business is all about," he said loudly, and his voice carried clearly across the night to the four children who stood, panting, in the shadows of the bushes that separated Aunt Alice's house from the hotel.

"We made it," Liz gasped. "He didn't see us." There was a note of triumph in her voice.

"No, he didn't see us," Bruce said quietly, "but there's something he *will* see. The cord's been ripped out of the projector, and it's still attached to the extension, and that's still in the outlet in the wall of the Bateses' house."

Chapter Fourteen

THANKSGIVING DAY passed quietly. It was a strange, still sort of day with the sky clear and blue and the cold of almost-winter settled over everything.

Debbie left for home soon after breakfast in order to share the holiday with her own family. The Walkers and Aunt Alice went to church and came home for the traditional turkey dinner. Then Mr. Walker brought in some wood and they sat together in front of the fireplace to enjoy the first fire of the season. There was no sound from the hotel.

"Preston must have settled down at last," Liz whispered to Bruce in one of the few private moments they had together. "He looked really at home there when I sneaked over this morning to take the dogs their breakfast."

"Everything's too quiet," Bruce said uneasily. "It's like the stillness right before a thunderstorm. It's a getting-ready sort of feeling."

His stomach felt sick and queasy under its load of turkey and dressing.

"The projector cord is gone out of the outlet. I looked over there after church. It won't be long now before Jerry brings his father over here, and they'll talk to Dad, and the whole story will be out."

"I don't think so," Liz told him confidently. "Just having the cord won't tell them where it came from. They'll guess how the ghost trick worked, but they won't know who did it. If they do come over, all we'll have to do is act like we don't know what they're talking about."

"The projector's smashed," Bruce reminded her grimly. "Do you think Dad's not going to notice that? Especially when the cord's torn out of it and a matching cord has turned up in the Bateses' wall?"

"Stop worrying, Bruce. It's Thanksgiving. We have scads of things to be thankful about." Liz would not be depressed. "The whole thing worked perfectly. Just hearing Jerry scream — wasn't that worth anything? 'Help! A ghost! A ghost!'" She giggled at the memory. "And Dad's going to be working right here in Elmwood. Think how great that is. We'll be close enough to keep up the hotel. Imagine if we'd had to move again halfway across the country. What would we have done with the dogs?"

"I guess you're right," Bruce said, and he tried to feel thankful. But the cold, waiting feeling remained inside of him. All the rest of the day he fought it, but by nightfall it was still there as solid as ever. Something — and not a good something — was going to happen soon.

When the something did occur, it was the next morning. Liz knew it first. The doorbell rang just as she was clearing the breakfast things from the table.

"Who could that be?" she wondered out loud.

"It's probably the man from the real estate agency," said Mrs. Walker, drying her hands on a dishtowel. "When I talked to him Wednesday, he said he'd be over first thing this morning, but I didn't know it would be quite this early."

"You mean we're going to look at houses?" Liz asked her.

"We certainly are," her mother said happily. "Your father's Aunt Alice is a wonderful, kind, good, generous person and she has been marvelous letting us stay here, but, oh, Liz, you can't imagine how happy I'll be to have a kitchen of my own again!"

The man from the agency was named Mr. Crabtree. He was short and bald with a black mustache and a very precise, decided manner.

"Let's see if I have your requirements correct," he said in a businesslike voice, as he drew a sheet of paper from his briefcase. "You want a living room and dining room and a den with a fireplace. At least three bedrooms. A big back yard with trees and planting."

"That's right," Mrs. Walker said. "And if possible we'd like it in this neighborhood. I hate to make the children change schools again."

Mr. Crabtree frowned. "Well, that makes things a little more difficult. Most of the houses I had listed for you to look at are in other school districts. There's one, though, the Brower place, which might be just what you're looking for. Would you like to see it now?"

"Yes, indeed," Mrs. Walker said eagerly. "I'll get my coat. Can we take your car? My husband has ours at work."

"We won't need to drive," Mr. Crabtree said. "It's very close, just a short way down the street."

"It's *what?*" Liz felt a sudden chill sweep over her. "Oh, Mother, no — we don't want that house! It's old. It's shabby. The yard's all overgrown."

"Houses can be painted," Mrs. Walker said comfortably, "and grass can be cut, and I like old houses. They have a nice, lived-in feeling to them. Besides, how convenient it would be to live close to Aunt Alice! She could drop over and see us whenever she felt like it, and we could visit her, and she'd never feel lonely again."

"Mother, no. Please. Don't let's go over there!" Liz was almost weeping.

Her mother regarded her with bewilderment. "Of course, I'm going over there. Why shouldn't I, for goodness sake? Really, dear, this isn't at all like you. Don't you want to come with me? You've never seen the inside of it either."

"I don't — I can't!" Liz whirled and went tearing down the hall. "Bruce! Bruce! Where are you? Bruce, the thing you were scared of — it's happened!"

Bruce was in the den trying to study. He glanced up when his sister came rushing in. One look at her face was enough to drain the color from his own.

"What is it? What's happened?" He was out of his chair in a minute. "Who was that at the door? Mr. Bates and Jerry?"

"No, worse. Much worse." Liz could hardly get out the words. "A real estate agent's here, and he's taking Mother to look at houses, and the first house they're going to look at is *our* house! The dogs' house! The *hotel!*"

"Oh, my gosh!" Bruce was down the hall and out the door like a bullet.

By the time he had reached the sidewalk, he knew it was too late. His mother and Mr. Crabtree were already standing on the front steps of the hotel, and Aunt Alice was with them. Mr. Crabtree was fitting a key in the lock.

"It's a roomy house," he was saying. "Just the number of rooms you are looking for. The people who owned it had to leave suddenly."

"Mother!" Bruce shouted, and his mother turned to wave at him.

"Come with us, dear," she called cheerily. "We

may be getting our first look at our new home!"

"It's too late, Bruce." Liz echoed his own thoughts as she caught up with him. "It's too late to do anything now except pray."

Moving together, shoulder to shoulder like soldiers going to face a firing squad, they followed their mother and Mr. Crabtree into the familiar brown house.

The moment they were in the hallway, Aunt Alice started sneezing.

"How odd!" she said. "If I didn't know better I'd think there was animal hair around here someplace. I feel just the way I do when — when — when — atchoooo!"

"Bless you," said Mrs. Walker. "Perhaps it's dust. Although it does look clean, doesn't it, for having sat empty for so many months?"

"This is the living room," Mr. Crabtree was saying. "Natural wood floors, you'll notice. The master bedroom is on the first floor also. If you'll just follow me — " With quick, efficient steps he led the way down the hall toward the pink bedroom.

"I can't watch," Liz breathed. "Oh, Bruce, I just can't!"

She shut her eyes tightly.

A shriek split the air. "There's something in there!" Aunt Alice screamed. "It's — it's — atchoooo! It's a *dog!*"

"It's two dogs!" Mrs. Walker cried, as Sadie and

MacTavish shot past her and came racing down the hall to Bruce and Liz.

"Why, how incredible! How could they have gotten in here?" Mr. Crabtree blinked his eyes in amazement. "It seems impossible —"

From the floor above them a deep, melodious voice broke into a howl. It rose higher and higher in a mournful beagle wail.

"That's the sound we heard the other day!" Mrs. Walker exclaimed. "It's coming from upstairs!" She started briskly down the hall.

"Wait, wait, Mrs. Walker! Don't go up there alone." Mr. Crabtree came hurrying after her. "Let me go up first. It might be something dangerous." Pressing his way past her, he started up the stairway.

Liz choked back a sob. "They're going to find Preston!"

"And Annabel's pups." Bruce's face was strained and white. "But they haven't found Red yet. I'm going back to the den and see if I can get him out through the window. I'll hide him somewhere, even if I have to run away with him! They can't find him and give him back to Jerry — they just can't!"

Turning quickly, he ran down the hall toward the back of the house. At that moment another scream broke forth from Aunt Alice. Preston, followed by the five joyful Bulldales, came tearing down the stairs to greet his company.

"Oh, my goodness!" Mrs. Walker gasped, clutching at the railing to keep from being knocked over as the string of dogs shot past her. "Why, it's — it's like a — a zoo!"

"Believe me, Mrs. Walker, Mrs. Collins —" Mr. Crabtree appeared at the top of the stairs. His mustache was twitching nervously. "Believe me, ladies, I had no idea. I still have no idea. This has never happened before. Never at any house on our list."

"Atchoooo! Atchoooo! Atchooo!" Aunt Alice leaned weakly against the wall, helpless with sneezing. Her eyes were watering so hard that great tears rolled down her round cheeks.

"Oh, poor Aunt Alice!" Mrs. Walker rushed over to put an arm around the elderly lady. "Here, let me help you! Liz, come take her other arm! We have to get her outside!"

"Here, Aunt Alice! Lean on me!" A little frightened by the violence of her aunt's attack, Liz helped to steer the sneezing woman down the hall to the front door.

She really *is* allergic, she thought. She wasn't just making it up at all. No wonder she didn't want Bebe to stay with us. They stepped through the doorway into the fresh chill air, and Aunt Alice drew a shaky breath and wiped at her teary eyes.

"Oh, that was dreadful!" she gasped. "Just dreadful! All those animals! How did they get in there?"

"I don't know, dear," Mrs. Walker said. "Mr. Crabtree will find out."

"Indeed, I will," Mr. Crabtree told them. Not only his mustache, but his whole face, was twitching with outrage. "May I use your phone, Mrs. Collins? I'll call the Humane Society. They'll send a wagon for these beasts."

"But you can't do that!" Liz burst out wretchedly. "You can't let them be dragged off. They're nice dogs. They couldn't help being where they were put and having Aunt Alice allergic to them."

"Of course, they couldn't help it," Mrs. Walker said. "Nobody's blaming the poor animals. They have no homes and nobody to take care of them. I'm sure they're eager for any shelter they can find."

"But they do have a home! They are taken care of!" Liz cried. "Mary Ann Martin owns Preston, and I own Sadie, and Tim sort of owns MacTavish, now that he's gotten used to him. Annabel Higgins owns the Bulldales, and Bruce —" She stopped herself before she got to Bruce. "They're our dogs, Mother, all of them! They can't be lugged off in a wagon!"

"You and Bruce and Tim —" Mrs. Walker repeated in confusion.

"And Debbie too. She's a partner." Liz was really crying now.

"Elizabeth Walker!" Her mother's voice was low and controlled. "What is it that you are trying to tell me? I want the truth now, not one of your stories. Are you children responsible for this menagerie? Have you been keeping eight dogs here in this house?"

"I think the count is nine," a man's voice said quietly. "Look who I found headed down the street as I was on my way home to lunch."

Blinking back her tears, Liz saw Mr. Bates coming toward them along the sidewalk, and Bruce and Red Rover were with him.

Chapter Fifteen

I T TOOK MR. WALKER exactly ten minutes to get home from work after Mrs. Walker called him. Since his office was normally a twenty-minute drive away, it seemed to the children that the only way he could have made the trip so quickly was to have flown.

He still seemed to be flying as he leaped out of the car and strode up the walk and into the house. His face was grim as he glanced about at the little group assembled in the living room.

"What in the world has been going on here?"

"You'd better ask your son and daughter that," Mrs. Walker said as calmly as she could. "It seems they have turned the vacant house down the street into a kind of dog hotel. There are nine dogs there now; at least, there were at the last counting. One of them happens to be the Bateses' long-lost Irish setter."

"A dog hotel." Mr. Walker repeated the words

as though they had been spoken in a foreign language. He turned to Bruce, who was seated forlornly on the end of the sofa. "What's all this about, son? I think you'd better come up with an explanation."

"Well —" Bruce said slowly. How exactly had it all started? "I guess the beginning was Sadie."

"Sadie is mine," Liz said. "At least, I was the one who found her. It was raining, and she ran in one night while you were dripping on the carpet, and she had puppies upstairs in the sewing-room closet."

"She had puppies *here?*" Aunt Alice gave a startled gasp. "There were a dog and puppies right here in this house?"

"We got them out as fast as we could," Liz said. "We didn't want to start you sneezing. And then when Bruce found out about the vacant house and that Jerry Bates had knocked out the windows —"

"He *what?*" Mr. Bates, who was seated in the armchair by the window, straightened up with a jerk. He was a big man and handsome like Jerry, but there was a look of kindness in his face which could not be found on Jerry's. "My son, Jerry, broke windows? Why wasn't I informed?"

"I didn't think you'd believe it," Bruce told him. "Tim Kelly said you never believed anything bad about Jerry. But the windows *were* out, and the house was empty, and when Red ran away and we found him —"

"— and he was hurt and scared," Liz said, "and he loved Bruce —"

"— and then Liz and Debbie came home with MacTavish —"

"— and the Bulldales were going to be drowned —"

Once they were started, they could not stop themselves. The story had been building within them for too long. Now out it came, pouring like a stream rushing down a mountain. By the time they were finished, Liz was crying again and Bruce was biting his lip to keep it from quivering.

"Preston, the beagle, was our only paying guest," he ended. "Mary Ann Martin's father is paying a dollar a day for us to keep him. We needed money dreadfully. The food costs have been high."

"I imagine they have been," Mr. Walker said wryly. "This sounds like a pretty expensive enterprise. Nine dogs is hardly a small family."

"It's more than just food," Liz said. Now that things were out in the open, it seemed that he might as well know the worst. "We have to pay to have your projector repaired. It's smashed, and the cord's gone out of it."

"That cord was from your projector?" Mr. Bates broke in. A light of understanding came into his eyes. "Things are beginning to fall into place now. You wouldn't happen to have a color slide of Red Rover anywhere around, would you?"

"Yes, sir," Bruce said miserably. "It's in my jacket pocket."

"Bruce is a wonderful photographer," Liz said. "The picture looks just like Red."

"Jerry thought it did also," Mr. Bates said shortly.

"The thing as I see it," broke in Mr. Crabtree, "is that this is a clear case of breaking and entering, of damage and vandalism —"

"I hardly think that," said Aunt Alice. She spoke in a calm, decided manner, very unlike her usual nervous flutter. "The children did not break, they merely entered. The breaking had already been accomplished. As for damage and vandalism, I certainly didn't see signs of any. The inside of the house was clean and in excellent repair."

"That is hardly the point," Mr. Crabtree said coldly. "As I see it —"

"A house standing open with panes out of the windows," Aunt Alice continued as though she had not heard him, "is an open invitation to children. It is what is legally termed 'an attractive nuisance' and is the owner's responsibility. The only possible charge that might stand up in court is trespassing."

She paused. Then, seeing the confusion on Mr. Crabtree's face, she continued in a gentler tone. "My husband was a private detective, and I worked with him and ran his office for many years. We had many fascinating cases and were in court a number of times. I have a good fund of legal knowledge."

"Aunt Alice!" Liz regarded her father's aunt with astonishment. "You never told us!"

"You never asked, dear," the little white-haired woman said placidly.

"Well, trespassing then. That's bad enough," Mr. Crabtree said. "What if I had taken another prospective buyer to see the house? How could I have explained all of those animals leaping out from all directions? I would certainly have lost a sale, and my client might even have had heart failure."

"But that didn't happen," Mrs. Walker reminded him. "Nobody had heart failure. And you didn't lose a sale. In fact, I think you may have made one."

"The point is —" Mr. Crabtree stopped in mid-sentence. He stared at Mrs. Walker. "Pardon me? I don't think I quite understood you."

"I said, you may have made a sale." Mrs. Walker turned to her husband. "It's really a lovely house, dear, with nice big rooms and two baths and a fireplace. With some hard work next summer, the yard could be made beautiful."

"The location is good," Mr. Walker agreed. "It's close enough to my work and near Aunt Alice. I'm willing to take your word on the inside being what we want. If the price is right for us —"

"I'm sure it will be." Mr. Crabtree looked as though a miracle were happening. "The owners are very anxious to sell, especially since they don't live close enough to keep the place up."

"Of course, we wouldn't be able to buy at all," Mr. Walker said, "if we had to pay a court fine for trespassing. I have to agree with my aunt that *that* charge is justified."

"Oh, I don't think the owners will press charges," Mr. Crabtree said quickly. "In fact, under the circumstances, I can see no reason for even telling them. Since the property in question will be yours soon anyway, we can just consider that the children were 'looking it over.'"

"Which brings us," Mr. Walker said, "to the next issue: the dogs."

"I guess you're going to make us get rid of them," Liz said mournfully.

"I guess I certainly am." There was no sympathy in her father's voice. "Nine dogs, and then Bebe! You do still want to keep Bebe, I take it?"

"Of course I want Bebe!" cried Liz. "I love Bebe! I wouldn't give her up for anything. But I love Sadie too, and they would have such good times together, and there's so much room at the hotel."

"Two dogs." Mrs. Walker spoke softly. "That's not so terribly many. I had two dogs when I was a little girl."

"Tim will take MacTavish," Bruce said. "I'm sure he will. And Liz and Annabel are training the Bulldales for the circus. Though," he added with honesty, "they haven't learned any tricks yet. They're funny, but they're not very smart."

"We're not going to keep them until they do learn," Mr. Walker said decidedly. "Tomorrow we put an ad in the paper. Christmas is next month, and people always want puppies at Christmastime. You'll pay for the ad too, you kids, until every last one of those animals is gone."

The telephone rang. Aunt Alice went to answer it. When she came back she said, "It's for Liz. A lady."

"If it's someone with a dog," Mr. Walker said, as Liz got up from her chair, "don't you dare tell her we'll take it."

"I'll pay for the ad, Dad," Bruce said. "I'll pay to have the projector repaired too. I've got money put aside. I was saving it —" He swallowed hard. "I was saving it to buy Red from the Bateses."

"And what made you think that dog was for sale?" his father asked him.

"I didn't. I mean, I knew he wasn't. I just —" Bruce looked down at the floor. He could not meet his father's eyes. He did not want anyone to see that his own had tears in them.

"He wasn't for sale at that time," Mr. Bates spoke up from his chair. "But he is now."

Bruce raised his head. "What did you say, sir?" he asked incredulously.

"Red Rover is for sale," Mr. Bates repeated firmly. "Jerry isn't ready for the responsibility of a dog. When a boy wakes at night to a ghost, he can come out with confessions he would never think of making in broad daylight. I learned a lot about my son that night — a lot that I should have known before."

He shook his head sadly. "I should have listened. People tried to tell me. I should have opened my eyes. It's just that when it's your boy and you love him, you don't want to admit to yourself that he's less than perfect."

"We're all less than perfect," Mrs. Walker said. "Children have to be taught the rules of living. There are a lot of them that our two haven't yet learned."

"But they know the basic ones — kindness and

sharing," Mr. Bates said. "Jerry doesn't, and it's not entirely his fault. He's an only child, and his mother and I have tried to make that up to him. We couldn't give him a brother or sister, so we've kept giving him *things*."

"Red isn't a *thing*," Bruce said. "He's a super dog. He deserves a super home with a super master."

"He does," Mr. Bates agreed. "And I'm going to see that he gets one. Would you still like to buy Red Rover?"

"I can't afford it," Bruce said miserably. "I owe so much money already."

"I'd be willing to wait for payment," Mr. Bates told him. "The main thing now is knowing that Red Rover is being loved and cared for."

"Dad? Mother?" Bruce turned to his parents beseechingly.

"Three dogs —" There was doubt in his father's voice.

"It's better than nine dogs," Mrs. Walker reminded him.

"Guess what, everybody!" A voice spoke out from the doorway. It was a funny, choked-up sort of voice that seemed to be trying to keep itself steady. "Guess who you're looking at."

There was a moment of silence. Then Mr. Walker said, "Why, we're looking at a girl named Elizabeth Walker."

He tried to speak lightly, but the words came out

sounding strangely uncertain. The girl in the doorway was pale, and her hands were clasped tightly before her. She looked like a person just waking from a dream.

"You're looking," she said, "at Elizabeth Walker, the published writer."

"Liz!" Mrs. Walker gave a cry of delight. "You don't mean it! You've sold a poem?"

"Miss Crosno did it," Liz said in the same funny voice. "I turned it in by mistake one day. Miss Crosno didn't tell me, but she submitted it to the school paper. They're going to publish it in the Christmas issue. It's always the sixth graders who write for the paper. They've never used a poem by a fifth grader before, never ever in the history of the school!"

"But they won't pay, will they?" Bruce regarded his sister skeptically. "I thought the whole idea was that you wanted to earn money."

"Money?" Liz said blankly, as though she had never heard of the word. "Why, there are years ahead for that." Suddenly she was the old Liz again, chattering and laughing.

"This is the beginning, Bruce, just the beginning!" Her eyes were shining like stars. "I'm one week short of eleven! I'm already ahead of Shakespeare!"